tools and materials, wish their fellow artists a good night, and climb up onto my suspended body. Each and every one of you rest prostate on my torso, close to one another, and sleep the sleep of the safe and innocent. My sunken chest forms a huge bowl which I fill with water. If one of my fellow artists should wake up thirsty they can lap at it like a little cat. Come daybreak, hands with spans of spades softly stroke your hair. Roused, you hear my voice, deep and dark but gentle and measured, whisper "Wake up!"—upon which clarion call each new day would begin.

My willing yield of body and mind eventually exacts its toll. My complete acquiescence to your comfort eventually exacts its toll. Over the years my joints begin to calcify and my cartilage perishes like stringy rubber bands. My skin is here pale and translucent, there sags and puckers. My grip begins to weaken, the hammock that is me begins to droop, and you begin to feel uncomfortable. I slowly lower myself and my passengers to the ground as my wrist bones and ankle bones splinter like stick-rock candy. As you dismount, the patter of footsteps on my ravished body ripple my spine and snap my neck. My head rolls completely off its shoulders.

The spin-cycle of my consciousness fades and I welcome my expiration, happy in the conceit that I expressed my grateful sentiments.

Rhetorical Grimace

Joanne Tatham

Hello how are you? I missed you.

Did I tell you that I once had dinner with Carl André?

Did I tell you that sometimes I get picked up and sometimes I get picked up and they take me right around the block? It's a good thing I like to travel.

Sometimes I wake up screaming. What I see, what I see… I see an image of myself that is precise and detailed. It's terrifying! I mean I occupy quite a vulnerable position I suppose… not that you'd know that to look at me. It's a good thing I like to eat out. I like to eat out and I like to meet new people. I'm quite gregarious. I like to get involved. What do you do?

Listen, I can't offer the necessary exchange of accreditation and value as outlined in paragraph whatever, but you've got to remember, I am an item

disregarded in conjunction with previously agreed
expectations. I am a conflation of the deeper realms
of a psychologically fragile subjectivity and a strong
and certain attempt to create a rational, knowable and
justifiable account of the world!

You should tell me about yourself. I like to listen. Did I
tell you that I once met Franz West? I mean, who hasn't?
I admit I'm a dead weight, I mean I'm very heavy matter.
I like to sit in cardboard boxes and sometimes I get
picked up and sometimes I get picked up and taken right
around the block.

Did I tell you that I'd like to meet someone who shares
my passionate curiosity for life? I'm not sure that you'd
know that to look at me.

I'm usually available for examination by appointment
and will provide an unambiguously engaged response
to your probing, groping, prodding and all the other
manifestations of your obscene enquiry. Dirty shit. Stick
your fingers in my ears, if you dare! Stick your fingers in
my eyes, I mean poke them out!

Did I tell you that I once got caught in a damp, dark,
dank place? I don't like to talk about it now. There were
some dire circumstances and there was very little hope.
It's only to be expected though isn't it? It's par for the
course, whatever that means. Sometimes I get picked up
and taken away and sometimes I don't come back. It's a
good thing I like to travel!

I may arrive unannounced and interrupt you in a
manner that confounds the delicate balance of our much
anticipated relationship. Well, let's hope so! Did I tell you

I once met... did I tell you I once... did I tell you?

Listen, you should know that sometimes I wake up screaming. Sometimes I wake up hallucinating, shouting. I see visions of myself in which I am aware of the profound reiteration of verisimilitude that was previously deemed a necessary counterpoint to my fragile presence.

Did I tell you that I like to get picked up and packed up and shipped on to the next place? I like to get wrapped up. I like the sound the packing tape makes as it stretches off the roll. I like the polystyrene chippings and the layers of synthetic sheeted foam. I like to hear the screech of the screws that secure the lid! I should tell you... I should tell you that detailed instructions got misplaced in an exchange of emails dated sometime between Oct 3rd 2010 and a date as yet to be determined. At this point in time I remain damaged and somehow incomplete. How are you though?

I have begun to lose any unnecessary accoutrements. My non-essential elements will not recreate the previous assimilations of affect. I should advise you that I might require the attention of regulated experts. Well, what did you expect? I juxtapose my own disjunction in alliance with partners in international exchanges of commerce, trade and culture. I also provide my own bedding. Did I tell you I missed you? Did I tell you I once had dinner with Thomas Schütte?

I am all too aware of the rhetorical grind that accompanies the path towards veracity. Did I tell you I wake up screaming in the night? Did I mention that it smells bad down here?

I am an item... I am an item held in some regard by fetishists of a certain age and class. I think they're shits and dirty fucks, I mean, who doesn't? I would like to meet someone who shares my passionate curiosity for life! What do you do? I mean, I like to travel, I like to get about, I like to sit in cardboard boxes, I mean who doesn't?

4

Jesper List Thomsen

It is quiet.
The sun is hot.
The subway passes underneath, making the ground respond.
And again.
And again.
Step back.
My shirtsleeves are folded to elbow height, my Reeboks are worn.
Here and now we want nothing to be other than it is.
To think I need to move.

Copy copy copy.
Are you okay sir, do you need anything.
No.
In here it is a human sprawl, a theatre of all kinds. A classic situation rehearsed over
centuries.
A quadrel horizon obstructed.

A Keira K licking away on her Coco Mademoiselle.
A plastic bag reinterpreting what plastic bags do best.
Gently lifted from the ground for then
to fall again.
On falling.
A delicate gravity versus a north-western wind.
Walking in the shade with my mind on the ground.
Seven tall girls waiting for an audition.
Base.
Base.
One of these days.
Yellow.
Yellow.
Green.
Red.
This is part 4 where are we at.
The pavements are getting wider, I sense an exclusive air.
An older folk with cool sunglasses.
Two A's leaning against a white container.
A hole penetrating the beneath.
I count my steps.
I count my steps.
Red.
What is it about sneakers and their soles. The current trend is kind of perverted ruffle, or sole
icing. Look at me, look at my shoes, look at the soles on which I rely.
Dear pavement I am just trying to cheer you up.
And here on the other side a certain monotony. A vertical monotony dealing in quiet
ambition.
It's beautiful.
It's beautiful.
Three men in white shirts open one door after the other, taking a seat, contemplating the

beast.
Be sexy.
Write.
I am exercising straight derive.
Obeying to the inevitable.
I am a silent member making my way north.
And death.
Is it allowed to laugh at death. Is it allowed to make use of that very human mechanism,
laughter, in the face of death. When it finds its way in slowly maybe not, but what about when
it arrives so sudden that its presence becomes one of brutal absurdity.
Do.
Do.
Be.
Be.
And stop counting will you please. You haven't made much and you wont make much. You
are not like them and you wont be like them. Even here in the land of prospect you are
fucked. I am sorry to say it, but you are fucked. But you don't care, you have stopped caring,
and good on you for keeping it real. I mean, no, I am not even entitled to an opinion. Hi, me
too, I am younger then you, a plain observation. I am leaner then you. We share skin colour.
1, 2, 3, stop counting, stop counting you fucking idiot, get on with it.
I am making my way north staying in the shade.
You are not old, but lived.
Such rigidness.
Have you got restrooms.
No I am so sorry.
Richard Prince

Wayward Nurse (Crashed), 2006 – 2010
Estimate $ 4.000.000 – 6.000.000
Would you like a drink sir.
Coffee, tea, soda.
Just water please.
Flat or sparkling.
Sparkling.
Christopher Wool
Untitled (P522), 2005
Estimate $ 800.000 – 1.200.000
I never had a penny to my name, so I changed my name.
Again, I never had a penny.
Mark Rothko
Untitled (red and orange on salmon), 1969
Estimate $ 3.000.000 – 4.000.000
Green.
Green.
Red.
Green.
Red.
Green.
Staying in the shade pretending to care.
Be clever.
Write.
White tulips.
Red tulips.
Yellow tulips.
Rose tulips.
A monotonous straightness.

And then down and dark and cheerful.
Base.
Base.
The kind of place where trains ride high and women sing out loud.

Of course I am romantic, how can I not be.
Shut up stupid.
Up here the world gets another kind of attention.

5

On belief.
118
454
496
122
I feel numb.

Perverted ruffle.
Flat smart.
Flat func.
High not shy.
Or maybe high shy trying something new.
Moderate perverted ruffle.
Flat open.
Half high retro.
Flat func.
Flat smart.
Finished my coffee.
Dumping my cup.
On circulation.
On navigation.
On Broadway.
On bourgeoisie.
On opinion.
The intensity of movement is immense.
On men with no breasts, but fabulous bras.
I follow him.
On women with a very certain confidence.

On falling.
Down, obviously, learning height.
On landing.
Hard.
Perverted ruffle.
I am looking up, it is.
From here just a collective hum.
And the prospect of infinity.
And what a ruin it is going to be, celebrated and explored to an unheard of extent. But all
knowledge must go, all collective knowledge must vanish, for this place to be of interest.
Excuse me, watch your back.
Perverted ruffle.
Sexy integration.

I don't want to say revolution, but rather, revolution, as a thing.
Unnecessary noise.
Moving again.
It was really suitable for the post-war.
And a view of the west.
The hunter girls are chilling in the shade.
On straightness.
On ways of doing.
On Crosstown.
And an early moon.

A sense of relief settles in my mind, again I am a dilettante.
Again I am a dilettante.
I am faced with a rock.
And presidents of the United States of America.
More whites here then normal.
You wonna know what I want.

Perverted ruffle.

6

I am not quite there yet.

This is the furthest south I have been.
A beginning with two names.

It is 3:27 p.m., I am at the Tribeca Grand.

And what do you write when you have nothing to say.

When purple cups and cigarette butts make up your material. When the spectacle that draws all the attention is a cage being elevated to the 22nd floor. When it falling down, killing a few, would for sure make the headlines. When people speak in languages you know all too well. When she is a thing of beauty and the rest a bore. What do you write when your head is suffering from self-inflicted pain. When you feel alienated by familiar faces and strange manners. When you have gone off track and lost sight.

When the world has some catching up to do and no one seems to care. When you want to write in a language so simple that the signs don't add up. When you are back on track realising those horizons are in fact only a consequence of height. When you want to look look and stay quiet. When you know that you know that the qualities you appreciate don't make it here. When standing around sleeping is the only option.

What do you write when base is your favourite word.

What do you write when base is your favourite word.
When looking down appreciating shoelaces over faces.
When the graphic impulse is blown out of proportions.
When straightness seems the rule.

What do you write when technique is superior. When
stupidity shines. When glossy pants is doing rounds.

What do you write when a simple painting makes sense.
When men are making their way north. When you are
fully covered but short a quarter.

What do you write when your coffee is strong and
smelling fine. When girls are chatting sharing lunch.
When apples are wrapped in ways that saturate their
beauty. When people on their phones seem to be
speaking just to themselves. When idealism is banned
and no one knows where to go.

What do you write when the tension in your head is
moving on. When awareness shifts and you suddenly
start to care. When sanity prevails and things slow down.
When all the brave faces of this street stop doubting their
project. When women are wearing hats that support my
beliefs and men are trying to shift old literature.

What do you write when word upon word looks a waste.
When it manifests a presence but ordering is hard.
When bread is sliced. When beauty looks your way while
waiting for her salad getting dressed. When you pick up a
wifi but the page refuses to load.

What do you write when a leather jacket suits someone
and makes that one look hot. When pigeons indulge
in the muggy shit that makes up the profound. When

a symmetry of taps makes a lot of sense. When epic
is the buzzword and texting it to 78247 might make a
difference. When several greys come together and turn a
surface into an experience.

What do you write when queues are made up entirely of
people who don't belong. When architecture shows its
true face and exercises terror and triumph concurrently.
When the cold arrives and you pull up your hood finding
comfort in its informality.

What do you write when men are puking into plastic
bags. When blue turns red turns green turns yellow.

What do you write when topless men mingle with horses.
When faced with a spring green forest. When you have
come to the end and are meant to leave. When monotony
is the favoured means and simplicity your hideout.

Massacre of Ndi Igbo in 1966: Report of the Justice G.C.M. Onyiuke Tribunal

Luke Williams

Bent over desk, right foot on carpet, left leg crossed over right. Pale light on carpet from lightbulbs set into ceiling. Lights also reflected in windows to right. Trees outside moving in wind and tapping window. Head quite still, reading *Report*: The Nigerian civil war ended thirty years ago. In this long time memories have started to grow dim about what really happened.

Sits back in chair, spine resting against chairback, glances up from *Report* to windows. Reflection of lightbulbs bright on dark glass. Reads: To correct this historical blunder, we are forced to issue the report to the G.C.M. Onyiuke Tribunal of Enquiry which sat in Enugu from December 1966 to June 1971.

Uncrosses legs. Glances up from *Report*. Unseen rubbish moves on paved way unseen. Innumerable books to right on numerable but uncounted shelves. Sits up in chair, reads: 26th Witness. I am a native of Ojoto. Katsina is

perhaps the area worst affected by the disturbances. It was about 2 - 4a.m. in the early morning of 29/6/66 when a large number of Hausas burst out from the palace carrying sticks, machetes, daggers, axes etc. and all other dangerous weapons, spread themselves all over the town looting and burning houses and shops. My two big shops and stores were all looted as well as my residence. Not a pin was left for me.

Stops reading. Sits up in chair. Glances at windows then back to *Report*, onto which light falls and from which same light reflects. Sits back in chair, spine resting on chairback, left leg crossed over right. Reads: 16th Witness. As I understand and speak Hausa language very fluently, I had the opportunity to mix freely with every Northerner. What they were saying was 'NOTHING LIKE EAST WILL REMAIN IN THE MAP OF NIGERIA'. From this time onwards, peace and tranquility eluded Kaduna. I witnessed the heaviest killings, corpses were being transported from the town to the hospital. The extent of the killing was so great that the ambulance could not cope with the evacuation of the corpses so they had to employ P.W.D. and P. & T. tippers to help in clearing the corpses. The most sorrowful sight I have ever seen was that young men were sitting on top of the corpses dancing

Closes eyes. Opens eyes. Head turns right until eyes rest on row of shelves. Closes *Report*. Rubbish scrapes pavement, wind alternatively strong and light. Opens *Report*. Tries and fails to find last page read. Reads: 189th Witness. At midnight on the 22nd September, 1966, I was knocked out of bed by the troops who were shouting my name and threatened to blow down my house if I did not let them in. I came to the door in my wrappers and

without my slippers, I saw by the security lights that my house had been occupied by these soldiers. They were 15 in all. They were armed with automatic weapons. As I found that it was useless to refuse to open the door, I did open it and was immediately followed upon by three of the soldiers who pointed the weapons directly to my chest. I lifted my two hands

Closes then opens eyes in almost a single movement, reads: lifted my two hands above my head in complete

Glances right to windows. Tries to see beyond the dark glass. Trees tap window. Turns several pages forward in *Report*, reads: 29th Witness. What we heard was Ka-Ka-Ka. They were not aiming at anybody, just flinging the thing up and down. The first bullet got me here (forearm) as I was trying to run out. Another one passing hit me here (foot). Two persons already shot dead were lying at the door. I fell on them flat.

So, God gave me the sense. I just stretched my hand like this. The blood was just gushing. Half of my body was outside. I could not move because if I move they would know I was not dead. So in trying to shoot they got this leg (right leg). When they got this leg I did not know they got me at the artery. So, as soon as the bullet hit me, this leg died outright. I could not move and I did not want to move. I never knew that my artery or what they call tendon had been cut.

After they finished shooting, everybody was there just lying dead. We just saw blood rushing. You know Kano Platform is built in a sloping way like this. Blood was just rushing into the gutter just like rainfall. When they kicked their kit-car

Stops reading. Glances left to shelves. Returns gaze to *Report*, reads: When they kicked their kit-car they went away. There was no alternative than for me to use my knees. I crawled and crawled and crawled past all the rails in the railway station, under the wagons. I was there till half past three in the morning of 2nd October.

Stops reading. Eyes turn to windows. Wind calm. All quite still outside and quiet. Then wind blows hard again. Tree taps window. Returns eyes to *Report*, reads: Under this head we deal with what we consider the sinister aspects of the pogrom. The evidence disclosed that Northerners embarked on various methods of torture and humiliation. One method was described by the 72nd witness, Dick I. This punishment is one of the most dreadful ways of crucifying a person. A heavy rod is tied across the back or chest of the victim with his hands stretched and secured firmly on the rod. While the victim may still be standing on his legs, he is as helpless as a man nailed to a cross. In this position they then proceed to torture the victim by plucking his eyes, cutting his tongue or cutting his testicles

Closes eyes. Realises, at some point, mind has stopped taking in words. Rubs lids, bends over desk again. Opens eyes. Turns several pages forward, reads: 122nd Witness. By 7.30 in the evening we came to a village. They started to throw stones and shoot arrows at us. Our driver became nervous but he managed to pass the place with speed. When we came to a place further from the village in front, he stopped and was afraid to pass through the village saying that if we tried to pass they would attack us. The driver said we would wait until midnight so that probably by then they might disperse. We were there and somebody was riding a motorcycle going up and down.

Later on by 9 o'clock in the evening, we saw a pleasure car coming.

What town would this be?

Birnin Gwari. The car was coming towards us and we saw many people coming behind the car shouting 'Hi! ho! ho!' We became afraid. All of us jumped down from the lorry until they approached to about 30 yards to where I was. When I waved at them they shot me with an arrow on the finger.

Why were you waving at them?

I thought we could settle things amicably. As I was shot I took to my heels and went into the bush. There I pulled out the arrow and washed the wound in a stream. I wanted to cross the stream but it was too deep. So I stayed on the side. One young man saw me and spoke to me in Hausa. 'Namuni?'

Stops reading. Glances left toward rows of shelves, then back to *Report*. Reads: 'Namuni?'

Stops reading, pauses, reads: 'Namuni?' and I answered 'stet.'

Rises bodily from chair, turns left toward shelves. Searches nearest row, then second nearest left, then third nearest left. From fourth row takes out a thick volume and holds in two hands. Opens volume, consults one page, then a second page. Pauses, turns with volume still in hands, returns to desk. Places closed volume on desk beside open *Report*. Sits back in chair, reads: One young man saw me and spoke to me in Hausa. 'Namuni?'

Massacre of Ndi Igbo in 1966   173

(Are you for us) and I answered 'stet' (I am for you). So he raised a stone to throw at me. I asked him why he should do that; what did I do to him. He asked me to give him money. I gave him £1. He demanded more; I gave him 10s; he demanded more; I gave 10s. Altogether I gave him £2. Then he felt satisfied. I decided to go on my own to look for a lorry. When I got to the road, I saw some ten of them. They held me. I told them that I had given money to one of their relatives. They asked me to bring the remaining money. As I was trying to bring the money, they took away my hand from my pocket, opened my trousers, looked for money there. They searched for it in my drawers, tore it off, took all the money I had in my drawers and then they poured petrol on me and lit it. I fell down.

They poured petrol on you?

They poured petrol on me, Sir.

So you were on fire?

They poured petrol all over my head and face and lit a match. Then, I became unconscious and did not know what I was doing. It took time for me to know what I was doing. After a few minutes, the fire went off. I stood up, and they were looking at me. I told them that they could finish my life at once instead of burning me and leaving me half-dead. They asked me whether I wanted them to finish my life. I asked them whether I was the person who told them to pour petrol over me. They told me to show them the rest of my companions. I said 'no.' Then I crept into the bush and told those people in the bush that I was poured with petrol. I urged them not to come out, and

that they should tell people at home what happened to
me. I went back to the road.

Later on the Hausas came back. They saw I was not dead
and one young man started to hit me with a stick on
the neck. I looked up and saw him. He struck me again
and told me that they meant me to die. I said 'May God
forgive the Hausas for they do not know what they are
doing. May God bring unity to Nigeria.' One told me:
'Shut up.' that I would be killed. But one elderly man
said: 'Leave him alone.' He asked me: 'What is your
name?' I told him my name. He said: 'All right.'

Later on, they said that this man that refused to die will
be burnt with woods. They collected woods to burn me,
but the elderly man said they should not burn me. So,
they left me. One returned and continued to strike me
with sticks, on the back and the neck. After doing so, he
went away. I was surprised that I was still alive.

Stops reading. Glances right at windows through which
trees can barely be seen. Unseen rubbish moves on paved
way unseen. Trees more audible than visible. Returns
eyes to *Report*. Turns several pages forward, reads: I got
up and continued to trek. All that time, my leg was bent
because I could not go any longer. I saw a bridge and
went there to drink water. I saw that the hill there was
very steep, I managed to go down, drank and poured
water on my face, but the whole place was very dark and
the place was fearful and I was afraid that if I slept there,
I would roll into the water. So I decided not to hasten
my death, rather let it come from God. I wrote my name
there

Stops reading. Closes then opens eyes in almost a single

Massacre of Ndi Igbo in 1966 175

movement, reads: I wrote my name there, in case I should die

Stops reading. Sits up in chair, crosses left leg over right. Reads: I wrote my name there, in case I should die there

Stops reading. Reads: I wrote my name there in case I should die there or there or there or there or with God or on his knees or his bottom or his face or in fear that I decided with my two hands

Opens eyes. Stares at *Report*. Wind blows stronger, agitates unseen rubbish. Pale words difficult to make out on paper onto which light falls and from which same light reflects. Breathes in and out. On fifth exhalation bends over desk again, reads: Did your wife recognise you when she saw you?

Well, in fact, I was the person who called my name and it was through the information I gave that they knew it was me. They did not recognise me.

This is one of the worst experiences.

Yes horrible experience.

Thank you very much, indeed.

Have you started work?

Yes, I was employed in the Sub-Treasury, Awka.

All right, I wish you luck. Thank you very much, Sir.

Untitled

Jonas Žakaitis

"Some years ago my father told me about this thing that happened to him. So, he's driving back home from work, and it's late night already, pitch-black all around, and out of nowhere he sees this man standing at the side of the road up ahead, not hitchhiking or anything, just standing there. So my father slows down, rolls down the window and asks this man if everything is OK, if he needs a lift or anything? The guy looks at him as if he has never seen a fellow human being before, as if he just walked out of a cave. Yeah, he says, wherever you are going is fine. So they start driving and this guy starts telling his story. Apparently, my father explained, this man had said he was the owner of this huge furniture manufactory in our town, a very wealthy man. He had a big family, four kids, big house and everything. But then one day everything cracked. First thing in the morning he gets a phone call from the customs department saying that a routine search of one of his containers in the terminal had revealed that all the two-thousand-dollar replica Savanarola chairs he sincerely believed to be useless, but which would certainly sell well enough to a certain numb

demographic, had turned out to be priceless fifteenth-century artifacts and that he was guilty not only of a false customs declaration, but also of an attempt to export national treasures out of the country. And this was only the beginning. The second phone call was from his wife. As this is the last time I'm talking to you without a lawyer, she said, I just wanted to use the opportunity to say that you are without doubt, the biggest, lying dickhead I have ever met in my life, and don't even bother using your house keys again, I already had the locks changed. And then his business partner called, and then his friends. He tried screaming back at people, he tried asking what the fuck was happening and where all of this was coming from? He tried saying he was sorry, but all of that only appeared to make things worse. It was as if he was suddenly teleported to another dimension where everything remained ostensibly the same, except for the fact that in this parallel life he was the most cold-bloodedly degenerate liar ever known to mankind. Within a couple of weeks he had lost everything: his family, his business, his friends. He was friendless, clueless and basically homeless. In fact, he said, my father was the first man he met in months who would tolerate more than a five-sentence conversation with him. Of course, my father told me, he didn't buy any of the man's story, but being a good man and a man who likes good stories he took the stranger to a diner, bought him a meal, and they had a couple of beers together."

"And?"

"And then a weird thing happened. When they said goodbye and my father was about to get back in his car, the man got a ring off his finger, a serious gold ring, and started saying something about how he wanted to give it to my father, not to pay him back, but because he had no more use for the ring anyway and would only

be happier if this last souvenir of his former self stayed with somebody like my father, and so on and so forth. No way am I going to take this ring from you, was what my father said. But then the man started pleading and crying, saying that he had never wanted anything more than this chance to give the last gift he was ever going to give to someone. The whole situation was getting really freaky, so my father just said whatever, took the ring, threw it in his pocket and drove off."

"OK, now let me guess what happened next. Your father happened to be the next liar."

"Well, yes. Immediately when he got that ring the same deep black hole opened in front of him. A week later, feeling completely desperate he tried to find that man. Not knowing what else to do he waited for him day after day at the entrance to that furniture manufactory, sleeping in the park at nights."

"And found him?"

"No."

Shortly after Mother's Day I received the following letter from a lady in Florida who had purchased a set of bottles of "The Pope's Cologne" to give as gifts. I felt strangely and deeply touched by it and debated about sharing its content. I decided that I should. I think you will see what I mean. This is the letter:

Dear Dr. Hass,

I needed to tell you about what happened with "The Pope's Cologne." I ordered two dozen (24) to give out as gifts on Mothers Day. I came up with the idea after your interview on the "Sunday Morning" show, since my mother is a devoted Roman Catholic, I couldn't think

of a more appropriate gift for her and the rest of the mothers. We all had brunch that Sunday, six mothers in total, and I placed bottles of cologne on each one of the mothers' place settings. My mother was speechless and very grateful for the cologne and immediately opened it and (as she was making the sign of the cross) placed a few drops on her forehead and behind her wrist. She said; "It has a delicious and peaceful fragrance to it, I love it, very unique" and she proceeded to rub the small bottle as if it had magical powers. Throughout the brunch she was inhaling the aroma from her wrist and you could see in her eyes how much she enjoyed it.

A few minutes before the brunch ended we got the bad news that a friend of my parents for over fifty years had just died. He struggled with cancer but did not win the battle, he was seventy-six years old. The following morning at the wake, as my mother hugged his widow, the woman mentioned how pleasant her fragrance was. My mom proceeded to explain to her that it was a Mother's Day gift given to her by one of her daughters. The dead man's widow expressed a feeling of peace and comfort as she was hugging my mom, and said that it was the fragrance that made her feel this way.

So, my mom related the widow's comment with tears in her eyes and said that if she had only known the cologne was going to have this effect on her, she would have brought hers and passed it on to the widow. I remembered I had extra bottles of cologne in my car and I gave my mom one to give to the widow.

What I experienced later, I will never forget. The widow used the cologne to "anoint" her husband EVERY twenty minutes. She would sprinkle it on his hands, his head,

his forehead, and his neck. You could see in her eyes she had found a path to redemption through the cologne. Everyone was asking about the cologne and its origin. Everyone that came in to give their condolences could not stop asking about the pleasant aroma they were experiencing. Everyone was quiet and in awe for hours. She also kept on rubbing the bottle as if it was some sort of amulet or charm.

Biographies

Ed Atkins lives in London. He makes videos and writes – particularly concerning bodies enthral to technologies of representation.

Becky Beasley is an artist who lives and works in St. Leonards on Sea, UK.

Paul Becker is an artist and writer based in Newcastle upon Tyne, UK.

Matthieu Bulté is a brewer and a writer living in Vincennes, France.

Alex Cecchetti is an artist and a writer, walking in Paris, France.

Arjuna Cecchetti is an archaeologist and a writer based in Ulaan-baatar, Mongolia.

Simone Ciclitira was born in Trieste and lives next to Italy's deepest lake. He writes.

M Dean is an artist based in London.

Tim Etchells is an artist, writer and performance maker based in Sheffield UK.

Johannes Fa is an artist and writer, born in Amsterdam and working in the world.

Melissa Gordon is an American-born artist living in London.

Alex Graves is a writer and artificial intelligence researcher based in London.

Bruce Hainley lives and works in Los Angeles.

Nadia Hebson is a painter and lecturer based in Newcastle upon Tyne, U.K.

Fiona Jardine is an artist based in Glasgow and the Scottish Borders.

Allison Katz is an artist based in London and New York.

Valentinas Klimasâuskas is a curator and writer based in Vilnius, Lithuania.

Shana Lutker is an artist often based in Los Angeles.

Nicholas Matranga is an artist working and traveling in the Benelux.

Katrina Palmer lives in London. She writes, reads and installs recordings as a form of sculpture.

Siôn Parkinson is an artist and writer based in Edinburgh.

Francesco Pedraglio lives in London where he writes and tells stories through objects and videos.

Heather Phillipson is an artist and poet living in London.

Kit Poulson calls himself a painter. Increasingly this has involved writing stories.

Chris Sharp is a writer and independent curator based in Mexico City.

David Steans is an artist based in Leeds, UK.

Joanne Tatham is an artist. She lives in Newcastle upon Tyne, UK.

Jesper List Thomsen born in Denmark 1978, lives in London.

Luke Williams is a writer based in London.

Jonas Zakaitis is a writer and curator based in Brussels.

Cadavere Quotidiano

Cadavere Quotidiano
Conceived and organized by Paul Becker, Alex Cecchetti and Francesco Pedraglio.

A Project X Project
Published by Project X Foundation for Art & Criticism
Edited by Shana Lutker

Project X Projects is an extension of the mission of Project X Foundation to provide platforms for critical engagement with contemporary art.

First edition, 2014
Design by Brian Roettinger
Printed at Bang Printing

ISBN: 978-0-9886694-3-7

Project X Foundation for Art & Criticism is a nonprofit 501(c)3 organization located in Los Angeles and is the publisher of X-TRA. Visit http://x-traonline.org

Project X Foundation is grateful for the support of the Andy Warhol Foundation for The Visual Arts, the National Endowment for the Arts, the Los Angeles County Arts Commission, City of Los Angeles Department of Cultural Affairs, Mike Kelley Foundation, and the Pasadena Art Alliance.

Table of Contents

9   PAUL BECKER, ALEX CECCHETTI
AND FRANCESCO PEDRAGLIO
Introduction

13   ED ATKINS
Warm, Warm, Warm
Spring Mouths
(Demux)

20   BECKY BEASLEY
Herbstfreude (Autumn Joy)

25   PAUL BECKER
Beneath My Feet, The Ground. The Ground

32   MATTHIEU BULTE
The delay

35   ALEX CECCHETTI
A Pro

39   ARJUNA CECCHETTI
Don't Think Twice It's All Right

42   SIMONE CICLITIRA
Me, No More

47   M DEAN
Nhn

54	**TIM ETCHELLS**	
	Anger is just sadness turned inside out	
63	**JOHANNES FA**	
	When Attitudes Become Form	
65	**MELISSA GORDON**	
	Dear Paul, Francesco and Alex…	
70	**ALEX GRAVES**	
	Tails	
80	**BRUCE HAINLEY**	
	Cody Foster	
83	**NADIA HEBSON**	
	Moda:WK	
88	**FIONA JARDINE**	
	my effects	
92	**ALLISON KATZ**	
	Morning Verses, 22/09/12	
94	**VALENTINAS KLIMÂSAUSKAS**	
	Dear Reader,	
96	**SHANA LUTKER**	
	Have you ever slapped a dead person?	
104	**NICHOLAS MATRANGA**	
	All Prices Are Delayed	
108	**KATRINA PALMER**	
	bone (cadaver)	

111	SIÔN PARKINSON CRABMEAT
126	FRANCESCO PEDRAGLIO J
134	HEATHER PHILLIPSON Guess What?
137	KIT POULSON The Death Of The Corporal, A Journey Without Luggage.
145	CHRIS SHARP The Angels in this Place are Unrecognizable
154	DAVID STEANS Letter #2 (Gratitude)
156	JOANNE TATHAM Rhetorical Grimace
160	JESPER LIST THOMSEN 4
169	LUKE WILLIAMS Massacre of Ndi Igbo in 1966: Report of the Justice G.C.M. Onyiuke Tribunal
177	JONAS ZAKAITIS Untitled
182	BIOGRAPHIES

Paul Becker, Alex Cecchetti, Francesco Pedraglio

Introduction

Cadavere Quotidiano
A daily mourning

A confined stretch of time.
A month.
Everyday a different corpse, a daily cadaver.
Un cadavere quotidiano.
An otiosity. A redundant belief system. A useless limb.
A dead person.
The ultimate abstraction... a subtraction.
So many writers to produce so many texts: obituaries, elegies, eulogies, epitaphs for the daily demised, for expirations, cessations, disappearances, beheadings and defenestrations of ideas, emotions, objects, images and movements.

Cadavere Quotidiano is structured as a straight anthology of writers and artists preoccupied with the lumbering nature of the object and its relation to the written word.

Organised through a hypothetical timeline, a fictitious and abstract month of the year, the collection of short stories, poems and experimental narratives is both a heterogeneous take on writing as-and-about objects, and a classic, anthological gathering of texts.

Blank page

Warm, Warm, Warm
Spring Mouths
(Demux)

Ed Atkins

And you don't seem to be.
And how could you be?
And no provision has been made for the casual life in casual, freshly-laundered bedclothes, trousers dropped to excessively conceal the ankles.

And pain exists in the concave.
And pain exists in the convex.
Allowing oil to puddle, importantly.
Allowing the camera to pan back to the groin.
(Certain skittering forms impressing the rainbow
   meniscus. Lifespans of a few bleak seconds.)
And there's a certain earthmover named 'Dispassion.'
Printed in an ersatz military typeface on the bright
   yellow muzzle—right beside the curled exhaust flue.
The 'Dispassion.'
 —Named after an icebreaker that used to clear those
   unnamed straits
   at the top of the world.

To allow for the blood to flow thickly;
   red one way and
BLUE the other.
Or to flatten—to medicate and temper the earth.

> And I'm here in this trench. The last trench,
> perhaps:
>
> I don't want to hear any news on the radio about
> the weather on the weekend. Talk about that.
>
> Once upon a time
> a couple of people were alive
> who were friends of mine.
>
> The weathers, the weathers they lived in! Christ,
> the sun on those Saturdays.

And this whole thing a concession, really.
A compromised surrogate for a REAL fucking experience.
— All hobbled legs and gelatinous irresolution,
   hauling itself inexorably through the murk
   by the will of some unknown coronary motor.
I say 'coronary', but I have no idea whether it even has
   a heart.
I say 'pulmonary' without the slightest clue what a pair
   of lungs would be doing down here.
Or a brain.
Or kidney-shaped kidneys, sensitive genitalia.
And what would these things be doing down here if not
   performing their anatomic
   function?
And what desires power it?
And where is it going?
And what will it bring back?

And where will we hide when it's back?
And what the fuck is it looking at? For?
And what will we watch while it's out?
And how might bioluminescent THRILL be understood as both generative and symptomatic?
And of what?
And how!

A description I remember of a Christopher Nolan film
   was that everything in it looked like a fucking gun.
That the camera moved like a fucking gun.
That the music sounded like a fucking gun.
As if heard down the barrel of a fucking gun.
That Leonardo Di Caprio looked like a fucking gun.
That he would approach his reflection and apprehend
   himself—with WILD ignorance—as a kind of
   fucking gun.

And that scene
with the playing card and the bullet.
Or that one
with the balloon and the bullet.
Or the one
with the apple and the bullet.
Beautifully scored, also.

And I mean to say that, I don't really know how to make
   a gun.
I could make a bullet, I think —
— and perhaps
   eventually come up with a way to propel
   the thing sufficiently enough to make a mark—
   perhaps even kill.
And I don't know.
And I can make educated guesses.

And I am in a relationship with guns.
— Of semi-intelligibility.
— A little one-sided, I suspect.
And I suspect that guns know a frighteningly large
  amount about me.
Their particular penetrative aspect, etc.
Never constructive—Always destructive.
As in, we'll never manage to put that playing card back
  together.
And guns don't work down here.
And nothing works down here.
Nothing save for that NASA pen
and the off-screen Bathysphere.

> This one goes out to the long, oiled cock of
> a rifle.
> The ornate, occult rifle and its occult subject /
> object proposition:
>
> **I don't want to hear any news on the radio**
> **about the weather on the weekend. Talk about that.**
>
> **Once upon a time**
> **a couple of people were alive**
> **who were friends of mine.**
>
> **The weathers, the weathers they lived in!**
> **Christ, the sun on those Saturdays.**

Black curtain dropped. More an accident than
  stagecraft.
'Here,'
And the semantics of presence are borne out as
  demonstrative bags of flour or sugar,
one or two sagging cod loin, held aloft —

or swollen, obsolete telephone directories —
swollen with the same name over and over: the name of the
ONLY PERSON THAT EVER REALLY MATTERED.
And a trellis of smooth, thick cabling across the floor.
A confounding of muscled tentacles
    and the thin, cheap speaker cabling dragged about
    by coelenterate and certain slow-waveform eels
    and the stiff, glowing pricks emerging from certain
    LOPHIIFORMAL FOREHEADS and the too-straight
    lines of scientific investigation, PHOTIC EMPIRICISM
    and the pasty gymnastic ribbons of jism.

—And me playing the role of the decrepit spider
    who most certainly belongs on the landing
    and not in the bathtub, at the terrible whim of your ghastly
    children.

A spider-web stretched between the trunks of the last
    two forest trees. The trees were loaded with snow, and
    the web loaded with the spider, which was smooth khaki,
    big as a football, with a black hourglass shaped across
    its heavy back, quivering a very little on the taut, almost
    invisible strands.

The web must have been spun since the last fall, for it was
    clean of snow, and glistening with adhesive as if it had
    just been extruded. Neither were there any husks in it,
    and had I not paused to recover my breath and admire
    the sparkling of the sun on the snow-plain
    beyond, I should never have seen the gigantic wheel-and-
    hub shadow thrust into the wood almost to my feet by the
    cold sun. I should have hung there like a cloudy stocking
    with a full cap of bushy black hair, before my cries had
    shaken off the last snow from the
    far reaches of the forest.

*The spider clutched the very centre of its trap. As
I stared, a claw reached from beneath the speckled
haunch and seized as with tortoiseshell pliers the next
coil of the spiral.*

   *With a sudden revulsion, and not wishing to see its
   face, or have it bounding across the snow at me on
   terrier legs, I plucked my revolver from my pocket
   and fired. The spider exploded with a soft thud,
   and like a firework showered its gold and vermilion
   contents all over the wheel.*

*The sun broke on the shambles of wrinkling tissues; golden
juice lashed away from it.*

*Gobbets of amber gum, rags of crimson flesh, black
plates thickly set with spines and thin brown sheets like
mica cascaded past, frosting and shattering in the cold.
Ginger, strawberry, and apricot: it was as though pots of
various sorts of jam had been flung across a
whitewashed wall. The bony forehead-piece studded with
its eight eyes in sets of two, the size of walnuts and clear
and unwinking as diamonds, glided over a hump of ruby
tissue and sank into the snow. The whole mess started to
steam and through the rolling clouds I glimpsed a portion
of the copper-coloured jaws still munching.*

This one goes out to you: slathered with HIGHLY-
factored sun cream, picking your way across the
beach, taking in the unwound, undressed bodies
scattered according to the geometry of sunlight,
two proud ellipses of yellow sand stuck to your two
tremendous buttocks.

I don't want to hear any news on the radio
about the weather on the weekend. Talk about that.

Once upon a time
a couple of people were alive
who were friends of mine.

The weathers, the weathers they lived in!
Christ, the sun on those Saturdays.

Excerpted, appended and re-edited from a text originally written as part of "Tomorrow Never Knows," commissioned by Film and Video Umbrella and Jerwood Projects.

DECEMBER 2012

Herbstfreude (Autumn Joy)

Becky Beasley

Six Years Earlier

It's not obviously about happiness, more the productivity of an unhappiness capable of making something separate from itself.

In the midst of so much noise something happened which finally silenced me. All the years of speech and exuberance rose up before me and I became mute once again. The sense of place became acute, as if I had finally become grounded. It began slowly, simply the sound of something moving, almost imperceptibly, in the next room. The walls formed and softened. The floors became dense and earthy. I no longer wanted to hide inside these boxes. I wanted the boxes to be rid of me once and for all. In my joy it was all I could do to keep from jumping out of the window.

I roamed about, pulling things at random from the shelves, piles and tubes in which they were stored. It was all so lonely and forlorn. No wonder things had become

so hopeless. I could see it all around me. The colour drained out before my eyes. It was all grey. Gloomy, dismal, sad. Was this all I had to show for my best efforts. It became incomprehensible. Finally I saw what my father saw. Nothing. No, worse than that: nothing much.

The horror from which I emerged that afternoon is indescribable. No, worse than that: pitiable. I was the most disappointing daughter in the world and this was what I had to show for all his patience and encouragement. It was all over and the relief was immense.

( )

What joy, and how lonely it is to feel this happiness. The dead air, the mute presence of this thing on the floor. It's the kind of oblivion which can only be reached at the limits of an unrelenting abstinence. After all these years, the unwavering belief. What madness. It doesn't even matter that what happened has come right at the very end. With a moments hindsight (for very little time has elapsed), how else would it have appeared. It is the hovering at the instant of being finished and done with it that is the joy. The search is over. I am alive.

( )

What to do. Now the question changes. What to do. What next. How can a move be made which would appropriately... No, not that. Rather, how might the most inappropriate move now be made. How to follow through on joy.

( )

The force of the noise had kept the silence at bay for so long that what was once silent was almost entirely forgotten. It's easy to escape in the city. There are so many things pressing at the edges that the surrender occurs smoothly and is quite comforting. One day it is easier to run than to remain. But the running doesn't look athletic, quite the opposite in fact. That's how it works. Something that is the opposite of effort is required in these difficult times.

If what occurred earlier were the result of an act of friendship, a sudden ending, exerted in space, out of desperation, what kind of thing was this? It certainly came out of something which in no way resembled an afternoon, although it was certainly an afternoon of sorts. If a stumbling block, emanating out of gloom and ridiculousness, was capable of producing something so stillborn, so hopeful, what else might be possible in its aftermath.

At once the space cleared is replenished with more of the same, alas.

( )

Six Years Later

Current happiness is causing such a lack of discipline that there is very little for which to account. The love now resembles only the first love. It's very clear, giving way not to thought, but only to frequent bursts of joy. Today, I awoke. Bursting with joy. The loveliest of feelings, shortly followed by a reminder that I had

other things to do, a few chores, writing. This swelling
is getting in the way. Where once the day was long and
arduous, ridiculous, now each one will easily slip through
my fingers if I let it. So much less can seemingly be
accomplished! The distraction manifests in the form of
a soporific vagueness. A new methodology—a kind of
grinding technique which I've been working on these
last months—seems to be the only way to maintain any
discipline at all.

( )

The room is different, the walls are firm. On reflection,
and despite appearances, much remains the same. The
books, mainly. The table, another constant, although
a different one now and my favourite to date, is still
littered with piles of papers, documents and seasonal
things. Autumn things again. Recent newspaper articles,
books I'm reading (or grinding, since the still act of
reading is not easy in this state), a few invites (finally!), a
file of current things to do, to grind, *Herbstfreude (Sedum
Autumn Joy)* in bloom. *Fairly trouble free, but watch for
mealybugs, scale insects, slugs, and snails, as well as bigger
critters, including deer.* No problem there, then. Postcards.
In the centre, a small brass cannon in two parts,
sunglasses, a watch, an ashtray from Germany bought
in a charity shop in St Leonards, a jar of sour gherkins
I grew from seed over the summer and am currently
pickling for Ben's third birthday. The first few I harvested
are by now pale, yellowing, the rest graduating shades
of green, the last of which went in yesterday still bright
green, floating.

The weather turned a few days ago, the autumn equinox
precisely marking the change from sun to rain. It's

raining now. *Herbstfreude*, whose name translates from German into English as *Autumn Joy*, is in bloom now. *Herbstfreude* is a herbaceous perennial, forming a clump to sixty centimetres in height, with fleshy, oblong, glaucous dark green leaves and large flat terminal clusters of starry deep pink flowers in early autumn, deepening with age.

2006/2012

Beneath My Feet, The Ground. The Ground

Paul Becker

It may have been two hours later that the donkey and Frenhofer arrived at the top of a slight incline in the road to find a dead child blocking the path. One could hardly ride over it, thought Frenhofer. The child was lying diagonally across the way and was half enclosed in great fat lumps of dried out clay, mostly bleached white now in the sun but with still some hints of moisture around the cracks. The clay was the same colour as the skin of the child, as though one thing had been born of the other; either it had exuded the clay in death (covering right side of face neck, chest, torso to midriff and finally enclosing hip and all of one leg and right foot) or the child had been pressed and sculpted from the raw clay. Impossible.

The donkey was munching a tuft of burnt black weeds near the corpse's head, indifferent. Frenhofer considered the child for a moment and then bent over to it. Not wishing to pull on the child's foot in case something happened, Frenhofer made a grab at the clay, but when he pulled it just crumbled off in his hand like a dry mud pie.

The foot revealed below was unusually translucent. After several abortions, Frenhofer walked back to the wagon and found a length of dusty rope. He passed a slip around the child's ankles and then dragged the considerable weight, clay heavy, to the roadside and away from the wheels of the truck. As he dragged it the clay shook, cracked and crumbled across the surface of the half child to which it adhered. Frenhofer watched fascinated as the cracks widened like fissures in the earth, mini boulders of clay cascading down onto the corpse's chest, dust rising as the mud turned to powder. He left the rope tied to the ankles of the child. The donkey was already moving off down the road.

For a while Frenhofer rode at the back of the wagon, looking back as the road slowly passed, his head was so empty he could hear it rattle as the wagon rocked. A neglected piggy bank, the last lozenge in the tin. No life passed apart from the occasional fly, bored of twitting the donkey or glutted with salt from its sweat, with the blood from its wounds. The sky was too blue to even contemplate, dreamless, no life there at all.

Some more time went by. Frenhofer went back to walking beside the wagon as the rocking had brought on more nausea. He stared at the ground. He drank a pint of warm water from the breaker after he had puked on to the road, the gulps and gasps loud in his ears. The donkey stopped again a bit further on when it found a strip of selfish shade under another lonely tree by the roadside. Frenhofer poured a few measures of water into a large tin bowl and let the animal drink. When it had finished, he placed the bowl back under the water keg, taking care to put a rock back into the bowl to stop if falling off the wagon. After a while of waiting, the donkey began to move again unasked and Frenhofer tried once more to

sleep at the back of the wagon, lying on his side, watching the wheels furrow up the dry dirt track, the sloughs of white dust and powdered mud.

Frenhofer was woken suddenly by a bump and a scraping of metal. Some sort of collision. Looking up he saw a black-faced and bearded man rubbing his eyes and looking out from the bed of another wagon. Both sets of wheels had jammed together, both drivers asleep. The donkey was sniffing around the behind of the stranger's horse like a dog. The horse was confused and a little startled even under its blinkers. Flies exchanging one beast for the other in a sudden frenzy of riches. Frenhofer and the black-faced stranger stared stupidly at the entangled wagons.

"You were asleep you idiot!' shouted Frenhofer, "What do you mean by trying to wreck my van?"

The black-faced man got off the back of his wagon and led his horse backwards by its halter. The horse was uneasy at this reversal. The man mounted back up, onto the seat of his wagon and geed-up his horse - a scrawny beast, almost a mule. All this time Frenhofer had been staring at him belligerently, muttering, and as he passed, the stranger lashed at Frenhofer with his whip. He missed, hit the donkey's rump instead and Frenhofer's wagon jolted away from the stranger who had already turned his face to the horizon. Frenhofer pulled up the wagon, jumped down and picked up a rock to throw at the stranger. He saw at a glance the man was too far away already but threw it anyway. If Frenhofer had a crossbow, he would've sent a bolt after this bastard, a bolt shot straight into the marrow of his spine, just to watch him dance about like a puppet, a beetle on its back. Frenhofer

forgot the stranger and his wagon and tramped along at the side of his own. The donkey stopped of its own accord a little further down the road and was watching Frenhofer suspiciously from over its shoulder. When Frenhofer reached it he punched its mouth. The donkey stumbled back a pace just a moment after the blow and then, well, that was it. It started to walk on again and Frenhofer jumped back into the driver's seat. A short time later, a box at the top of the load, presumably dislodged by the collision, cut loose and jammed into Frenhofer's back, leaving a bruise to develop over the next day or so. He retied the whole thing and then went back to walking at the wagon's side. The air smelt of chalkiness and was clammy and close. Clammy chalkiness. The donkey led them clumsily onward.

It was at the end of the third day that Frenhofer's work loomed up over the horizon.

What it was exactly was, to Frenhofer, all but an irrelevance. Even to talk about what he wanted it to be seemed like weak tea, too ordinary, or too prolix. He had been too long engaged in things: semblances of figures, surrogate humans like wax likenesses at Roman burials…

If a dog could sculpt a likeness, considered Frenhofer gulping down the last dregs of warm water, would it sculpt only other dogs or would it make its own cats: figments of desire encompassed. Frenhofer considered that to get to… whoever… whatever it, the work was, had constituted an act of considerable will power as well as the destruction of almost every other piece of remaining work. Old work. After all, what use was it? Bookends. Paperweights. Looking up at the distant

tip of it, Frenhofer could see... it was implicit even in that great unshapely mass... that an emptying out had occurred that should not necessarily be taken lightly. It was never just a voided bowel, more an amputation, an extirpation, a surgical procedure to get rid, to get rid of everything encompassed by what he did that he no longer required, would never find the life to make use of. Of course, the argument could be made that his oeuvre was always essentially reductive, he was a stock simmerer, a spring cleaner, filling buckets and bins until the void space behind the barn was packed with detritus, the dust of smashed plaster, wasted clay. But it was never easy to destroy attempts at something fine, something real. Frenhofer hated to throw away, to waste his time on applied failure, a pointless activity. Yet it had to be done because that, that was not yet IT, the *thing* and if not then what justification could it have in the world for existing at all? The donkey could smell home now and was picking up its pace a little, anticipating, what? a rest? food? Frenhofer knew for certain that the thing was right but not right and had to be destroyed to be continued. He must jump straight to it. A pick axe, a dull spade. Throw the wet clay back into the sack, unravel the armature!

Sometimes as he worked high up on the ladders the thing would in his mind begin a reveal, a shape would show itself. A strange form of anamorphisis, a boring Rorschach never before experienced and he was kept going for days in the misalignment of his senses that whispered he had hit on something. It would always prove illusory when he wandered off a thousand yards to look back at the thing itself: inauthentic, false, a cheap settlement made on the courthouse steps and the image would be slowly, painstakingly destroyed, remodelled, reworked with no sign remaining of its brief

manifestation. No sign at all. And so then, formlessness would take over, no man's land fought over so painfully, so irrevocably lost. He had eventually determined that the thing would be monumental, a mountain climb. He moved up in scale, the barn he began in was demolished around the work in progress like a Christmas wrapping, and the work gradually built its way out of the studio and into the open air. Now he gave more thought than anything to the simplest of ideas: the impact of size. Armature became architecture, the surface a series of tectonic plates, always shifting. Frenhofer secretly relished the inevitability of failure, somehow factored in to the narrative of the thing's construction. The possibility of it ever being completed. Frenhofer spent all he had on sand, cement and plaster, wire and wood. He had heard about a disused building over towards the city that was filled with old sacks of cement and had gone backwards and forwards many times with his wagon to collect everything that was usable. Sackcloth he had by the hundredweight to dip into plaster and fold over armatures. Frenhofer made thousands of sketches, all to little avail; the thing was almost too big for him to make an impact. That version too like a fat cloud, this one too much of a hideous mountain. He realised the process was flawed. This was not some bust that could be squared up from a drawing; the thing must learn itself, its own shape (or lack of) everything, all its formal dimensions and amplitudes from within. And yet Frenhofer carried on his sketches regardless, habits long formed, unshakeable despite all the evidence. He was trying to perfect a language he had never actually acquired. He soldiered on and sometimes, the inevitable false yearnings to finish, to succeed in his endeavour, to give the world his final work of finished genius, all of this overcame him and hurried the work along to the edge of yet another precipice, of

saying something solid and Frenhofer would have to hack his way back step by step to where he started from, to nothing, and the armature, then only twenty feet high, would be torn back, dismembered, curled plaster husks littering the floor of the barn like ribcages. He began again; wheelbarrows of plaster ran up the planks, dipping in hessian strips that made their way to the new cold summit and just as quickly back to the floor. Where did all the rubbish end up? He buried much of it in plaster pits dug into the powdered earth but the wind soon took care of that. Now they were just thrown loose to be blown where they would. He'd enough of piles; as though all he was doing was filling the earth with more shit, something else to be chipped away at, sculpted. And then what?

The Delay

Matthieu Bulte

Translated from French to English
by Barty Begley

He suddenly perceived through the smoke of his cigarette the hand at the top of one of the rocks that formed the horizon line in front of the water, at once vast and distant below them. He recognised almost in that same instant the end of the sleeve around the wrist belonging to the hand above the rock, and knew the identity of their owner, otherwise invisible behind the rock. His parted lips from which rose a hazy curl of smoke paled as they pressed together and from his nose came a brief thick cloud of smoke.

The cliff along the coast was divided by paths cut into the cliff to make the slope easier to climb, punctuated by steep walls with jutting rocks that made it possible to climb a out a few metres between the levels of the path. The surrounding area seemed deserted that day and the colour of the sleeve left him in no doubt.

The hand on the rock remained motionless, the fingers spread around the top suggesting a handhold while a

foot sought its next support. He considered that the hand remained motionless perhaps a little too long, that is to say that the head was taking a little too long to appear above the rocks. And besides he did not know if he had seen the hand appear, or if he had only noticed it all of a sudden.

The possibility which this motionlessness suggested to him, that the climber was in trouble, made him breathe out the smoke of his cigarette in a sharp breath, which entailed a slight relaxing of the shoulders, in its turn becoming a slight tilting back of the head, his nape barely but deliberately accentuating the movement: No chance! He'd never do me the favour. Fragments of their shared past rose to his memory, and the corner of his mouth that a moment beforehand had risen on his unmoving face fell back, to a little below the level of the join of his lips: Go ahead and die.

He perceived then a small dark shapeless stain on one side of the hand. This dark colour could be red on a particularly pale skin, blood from a cut on clenched white knuckles; the distant but powerful layer of sound from the waves could have covered a call or a cry; and he considered that he might not have recognised that the climber was in difficulty for having rather imagined it. The colour flowed along the ever motionless hand.

He stood up immediately as the still smoking cigarette fell from between his fingers, and in the same movement ran towards the hand, which suddenly slipped from the rock and immediately disappeared behind it, without a sound. A few steps later, he leaned out over the horizon of rocks.

There was no path beneath (the closest path formed a curve a little farther off, to one side), only a high wall of jutting rocks at the foot of which lay the body, whose contorted position vainly suggested movement.

The police (following his call) soon reached him from inland. Shortly afterwards a man from a nearby path arrived as well. The form and route of the other man's path had taken him away from the point of the fall as he came up the cliff after the accident and prevented him from intervening when he saw it. But this man had not only seen the climber in his difficult position and his fall, but also the man with the cigarette who had suddenly tried to intervene. His testimony confirmed that of the man with the cigarette, but he added (as particularly unfortunate) the following circumstance: that he had seen, without being able to make himself heard, the man with the cigarette look without reacting in what however seemed the right direction (that of the climber, or at least of his hand at the top of the rock) before suddenly running toward the climber and watching almost at that same moment his fall. At the end of this report, the eyes of the policemen who had listened to it came to settle an instant on the man with the cigarette, then turned away.

A Pro

Alex Cecchetti

I've been waiting so long that when the knock comes at the door I no longer know who or what I'm waiting for. And when I open the door behind that door is my father. I've had him come so I can kill him, now I remember. I let him in. I've been expecting you I say. I take him into a room just off the hallway. What do you want? he asks. In my hand is something as heavy as a stone. I take a good look at it, and it's a gun. I raise it and shoot and he falls down dead. Good, I say, good. I go out in the hall and a friend of mine is there. Kill him? Killed him. Good, he says. Good, I say.
I'm not dead yet, says my father's voice from the next room.
Didn't you kill him? Sure I killed him, I say, I shot him with this, and I hold up the gun.
I'm not dead yet, says again my father from the next room.
I go back in and the old man is still on the ground with blood oozing out everywhere and all that. His eyes are open, staring at me, his mouth twisted in a half grin, or a quarter grin. I'm not dead yet, he says. I shoot at him, two, three more shots, they echo through the room.

That ought to do it. Then I go out in the hall. All taken care of, I say. Now what? my friend asks. I don't know, let's have a drink. What? I don't know, anything. There's some wine, there must be some wine. In the kitchen, try the kitchen.

I'm not dead yet, says my father once again from the next room. I'm not dead yet.

What the hell? I say, this is starting to get to me. What do we do? I've got this friend, says my friend. A guy who knows what's what. A pro. Let's call him, I say. You call him, he says, it's your father not mine.

We wait so long that when the knock comes at the door we no longer remember who or what we were waiting for, just my father's voice saying the same thing over and over. I'm not dead yet. I'm not dead yet. He must be really getting a kick out of it.

I open the door and when I open that door behind it is the pro. He looks like Kenny Rogers, he looks like Chuck Norris, 80 pounds overweight, he looks like an egg with a beard pasted on, he looks like a fucking Humpty Dumpty with Kenny Roger's face pasted on. His fingers are far too puffy for a pro, I think. I'm the pro, he says, where's the job? I killed him, I say. With what? With this, and I show the gun. The pro makes a face just like my father's, and I could almost be tempted to blow his head off if it weren't for the fact that I need his help. For a job of this kind nothing does the trick like this, says the pro and out of his fat greasy bratwurst fingers pops a razor blade. Totally out of place held in amongst those bratwursts. You two wait out in the hall, he says. We wait out in the hall and he vanishes into the room. And from the hallway we hear the noise a razor makes slashing the jugular, and we hear the sound of breath hacked in two, and the sound of blood spraying or gushing out, and we hear the sound of shoes in puddles of blood shlack shlack and the sound of

shoe soles slipping in the puddles shlick schlick shlack. And the pro comes out into the hallway, raising his blood-soaked hands, and those bratwursts are holding the little razor, now all red and zincky. Powder room? he asks with a solemn look of satisfaction.

I'm not dead yet, says my father from the next room. I'm not dead yet.

The pro stands there with his hands still raised up, blood running into his rolled-up shirt sleeves, with the look of a total fucking chump. Give it here, I say, and take the razor out of his bratwursts, I'll do it myself, I say, and now I'm pissed, I mean really pissed. So I go into the room and my father is on the floor with his throat cut, blood coming out his mouth and all that and he keeps saying I'm not dead yet, I'm not dead yet. If I can't kill him I'll at least get him to shut his mouth. And so I squat on his chest and start using the razor to rip through his jugular, his oesophagus, cutting it all away and chopping, sawing, rooting out the cartilage, severing his vocal chords, and they snap like guitar strings and go glang drang, dilling dillang, dilling dillang and the room resonates like a sounding board. Sdilling Sdillang. And I feel the bone and tissue in my father's throat rasping against my skin and tearing wounds in my fingers, but I keep going until the old man's eyes roll around in their shattered sockets and his mouth makes vague grimaces and his teeth chatter and snap at the air.

HAYM NAH DEAH YEAH says my father.

HAYM NAH DEAH YEAH.

And he keeps burbling and rasping out hoarse words and spraying bubbles of blood from his trachea. Lucky me, I got friends. And Kenny Rogers comes into the room, with my friend, both with two pairs of shears and a light blue plastic bucket. They cut my father into bits, finger by finger, joint by joint, ankles, knees, ribs, ears, chunk,

chunk, chunk, all in little pieces. And each piece ends up in the bucket, the way that oysters, fish guts and pig innards end up in buckets.

HAYM NAH DEAH YEAH, says my father, then they cut out his tongue, his lips, his teeth, last comes his nose. They stuff everything in the light blue buckets, and there are nine of them.

Humpty Dumpty loads the nine buckets into his car, a light blue Dyane parked out on the dirt road in front of the garden. Inside the buckets, each little piece of my father is moving, jerking around, flailing in the blood and innards. They look like slugs, I say. Humpty Rogers says there's one thing a pro should never forget to do after a murder like this: hide the weapon. Then I remember I still have the razor clutched in my fingers. I show it to the others, and Kenny Dumpty looks at it with the air of a real pro who pays attention to the things only a real pro pays attention to. He goes up to a big tree standing nearby and effortlessly grasps it in his arms and lifts it off the ground. The tree has no roots and underneath the trunk the lawn is still a lawn as everywhere around. Throw it under the tree, he tells me, under the tree, as if were a doormat. I throw the razor under the tree, as if it were a doormat. The pro puts the tree back in place as if it were a doormat, then leaves with my father in the boot of his car.

This morning when I wake up I realize that I never filed my taxes, it's October and they were due in May.

Don't Think Twice It's Alright

Arjuna Cecchetti

**Translated from Italian to English
by Johanna Bishop**

Sara, not me, I mean the stupid one, was kneeling in the circle of light made by the fire. There with her in the same situation was Elisabetta. Kneeling with their hands and feet bound tight, arms behind their backs. They were right up next to the fire and trembling, whereas I was crouched behind the three-foot-tall metal drum, in the darkness beyond the circle of light. It was March 21, the spring equinox, and the night was damp and the sky overcast and the moon was a woolly sickle.

Like I said, not even five minutes had gone by since I'd got to that fire and I'd already figured out a lot about what was going on. They had got the wrong girl, and since things never go easier than when you're screwing up, they caught them and tied them up convinced that at least one of them was me. Instead I was there behind the drum with my rifle pointed toward the fire, because I had heard them talking and any time now they would be coming back into the circle of light. I kept an eye on

everything that moved and was in close enough range. Then they came back and as soon as I saw their faces I could tell they were morons, real morons like you don't run into every day. But unfortunately they were the kind of moron that can be dangerous. Like my dad says there are people out there who don't have a clue what they're doing and they can be vicious, really vicious, because they have no grasp of themselves, that's what he says. They were vicious and so I had to be quick and hope the right time wouldn't come too late. If you shoot at just the right time everything goes smooth, otherwise everything gets complicated and the trouble starts. There were two of them and I had to shoot twice but I didn't have two right times, there are never two right times in a row, there's only ever one, even when there are two targets and that's what makes things hard. I know it would be easier to shoot one guy, take a breath, take aim and shoot the other, but that's not how it goes. One of them told the other to bring him the redhead who he thought was me, but I don't have red hair, like I said, they were morons. My hair isn't even close to red. He said to pull her jeans down, too, because he wanted to teach me a lesson or whatever. That's what he said and I understood because they were talking Serbian which is the same as my dad's language, but the two poor girls didn't understand a thing and just started trembling harder and crying harder behind their gags. So I waited for the other guy to walk around the fire toward my side of it and when he squatted down next to Sara I shot the first guy, the one farther away and shot him right in the middle of the forehead. So now I had the one closer to me staring out into space with a silly look on his face, hunched over the girl like an ape, I lowered my rifle toward his chest and shot him and saw him go down backwards.

I was afraid he'd fallen onto the fire and it seemed gross to leave him there to burn in front of those two poor girls. So I went into the circle of light, slung my rifle over my shoulder, grabbed the guy by the hem of his pants and pulled him out of the embers, then took off. I don't remember what look those two had on their faces but I heard them crying and crying when I was already out in the dark headed home.

Me, No More

Simone Ciclitira

Damn you! he said, stiffening on the black wooden chair. The echoes of his voice filled the seconds, minutes at a time, minutes that became hours, filled every layer of silence that had accumulated since first setting foot in the house. Turning back, he gazed at the coloured lines interlacing, undulating on the monitor. From these shapes, he traced in his mind the corner of the room so many times seen before and while doing so, tried to rid himself of a fear that was beginning to control his body. The security of objects. The vacuum cleaner is usually there. Gazing at his desk, the eye rolling over (first of all) the newspaper clippings switching then to the bank calendar, finally coming to rest on the glowing penholder bought years back on holiday in California, as if concentrating on these details would allow him to force some sense of clarity.

How much time had gone by or how he had managed to turn around once again, he could not tell, yet he had done it. And still it took some time for the blurred, but undoubtedly human shape in the corner, to reveal itself as a boy.

The boy was sat on the floor with back almost completely turned away. He held his legs against his chest with his chin just resting on his knees. He was wearing pyjamas, which fit him as would the costume of a superhero, extremely tight, too tight at ankle and wrist, rocking back and forth on his small bare toes and heels, without ever turning his face.

Staring at the boy, he realised he could have done anything, could've shaken his head to try to get rid of what he was seeing or even screamed out in terror, but the more he thought about it, the less he could come up with a solution for such an absurd situation. He remained still and staring, hypnotized at that rhythmic rocking, that poised movement.

Then the rocking had stopped, the boy lifted his head and his face finally became visible.

Startled by the sudden change he dropped the glowing penholder, breaking the silence that appeared to be pulling them away one from the other.

The boy was no older than six, his cheeks reddened, healthy, as though he had been playing outside the entire day, his small mouth shut, firmly, expressionless. When their eyes met and he had looked closer at the boy, a shiver had run the length of his spine, penetrated, enervated his entire body.

At first the boy's irises had appeared yellow, as though belonging to a night predator. Then he realised they were a different colour altogether, but could not quite define it. They seemed to blur at the edges, like a TV with poor reception. Hiding something, revealing nothing. The boy

showed no apparent emotion, was apparently oblivious. Whereas, he, he himself felt increasingly ill at ease with having to deal with so many unknown entities all at the same seemingly endless moment.

Then, as if sensing his uneasiness, the boy turned completely around the other way, going back to his initial position, returning again to his rhythmic rocking. His chin was no longer touching his knees. His head was now leaning forward and kept hitting the wall in rhythm.

TOC TOC TOC TOC TOC
HEELS TOES HEELS TOES HEELS TOES

The easiest answer would have been to do nothing. Walk back to his desk, stare at the monitor and pretend not to hear that dull bumping sound.

TOC TOC TOC TOC TOC
HEELS TOES HEELS TOES HEELS TOES

He could wait for the sun to rise, hoping that the light would make the boy disappear, dissipate like a bad dream.

TOC TOC TOC TOC TOC
HEELS TOES HEELS TOES HEELS TOES

But no.

He maintained his place in the corner observing. Only a few steps separating the two of them.

The boy's body rocking rhythmically back and forth.

TOC TOC TOC TOC TOC
HEELS TOES HEELS TOES HEELS TOES

As the constant beating off the boy's skull penetrated his own brain he began to sense that something was changing. They were growing closer together. The walls inside the room were moving, getting further away from him. From beneath the terracotta-tiled floor a thick yellow carpet had started to appear, or appeared to appear. For the first time he also noticed a bed with a headboard covered by stickers and a big picture

window, becoming ever bigger, overlooking the swing seat on the edge of a large terrace .A far away voice was becoming clearer and clearer: 'Don't do that. Stop it!' He knew immediately the voice belonged to his mother. Instinctively he shut his eyes, squeezing his eye-lids tight, too tight, so much so, that when he suddenly opened them again, he was almost blinded, even though the only light in the room was coming from a miniature lamp.

The overall outline was once again this room in this house but that was the only thing that had returned to apparent normality.

TOC TOC TOC TOC TOC

HEELS TOES HEELS TOES HEELS TOES

Yet, nothing had really changed, at least this is how it seemed and after the dizzying sequence of events he had just witnessed and having got the boy back into focus, he realised that he didn't feel safe anymore, didn't feel safe now, sitting there in that black chair.

He got up and was now standing in the middle of the room. From there he could clearly see the boy's pyjamas stretching, his frail spine stretching back and forth each time he hit his head hard against the wall.

TOC TOC TOC TOC TOC

HEELS TOES HEELS TOES HEELS TOES

He inched even closer, now sitting just behind the boy. He hugged him, trying to stop the awful banging. As soon as the boy felt warm arms around him, he froze. The pleasant odour of the boy, a mixture of sleep and childish liveliness, of young life. He rested his forehead against the back of the boy's neck, placing his lips close to his right ear and whispering: It's alright now, there's no need for you to continue.

Then, all of a sudden, a thought came upon him, like one of his frequent migraines, the ones that fell like a stone, forced him to stay in bed all day, utterly unable to move, curtains drawn and sound of toilets flushing like a hurricane ploughing through his brain. His own childhood had not been sad; he had been a happy boy. My life sucks now, but not then, he thought. His jealousy and the falseness that was now characterizing the both of them had stiffened their muscles, compressing them. He had noticed by their embrace that he was giving off more heat and he wasn't about to let go. He had tightened his grip on the boy who was now beginning to fret and was looking for some sort of escape, sensing instinctively that there was none left, feeling trapped, drowning, at the bottom of some sea. Through the windows you could tell the air was turning from black to blue, light touching a little at a time, revealing to him the lifeless slender body that he was still holding tightly in his arms.

Nhn

M Dean

"Nnnh." "N" "Nhnn." "N." "Nnnhn." "Nnnnn." "Nnn." "Nnnnnh." "Nunnhn." "Nhnnhn." "Nhn." "Hnnn." "Nh." "Nh." "Nhhn." "Nnnnn." "Nh." "Hnn." "Nnnn." "N." "Nnnnhn." "Nhn." "Hnn." "Nnn." "N." "Hnnn." "Hnnhn." "Hnnnhe." "Hnnhe." Hneneh." "N." "Nw." "Nwh." "Nnnh." "Nhnnh." "Hnnnne." "N." "N." "N." "N." "Nn." "Nn." "N." "N." "N." "Nn." "N." "N." "Nn." "N." "N." "N." "Nn." "Nhn." "Nnh." "N." "Nn." "N." "Nhn." "N." "N." "Nn." "N." "Nn." "Hn." "Nh." "N." "N." "Nnnh." "Nnnh." "Nm." "Nhh." "Nh." "Nn." "N." "N." "Nn." "Nh." "Hn." "Nnnh." "Nnnh." "Nnnh." "N." "Nnnn." "Nnnn." "Nnn." "Nnn." "Nnh." "Nhh." "Nn." "N." "N." "Nn." "Nhhnnh." "Nhhn." "Nhn." "Nhnnhe." "Nhne." "Hnn." "Nn." "Hnn." "Hn." "Hnne." "Hnn." "N." "Nnnne." "Nnhe." "Nng." "Ng." "Nnn." "Nhh." "Nnnhe." "N." "Nnnh." "Nnh." "Nnn." "N." "Nnn." "N." "N." "Nnnh." "Nn." Nhhn." "Nn." "N." "Nnnh." "N." "Nnn." "Nnh." "Nnhnn." "Nnnhn." "Nn."
Nnn." "Nnnnn." "Nnn." "Nnnhn." "Nnn." "N." "Nhn." "N." "N." "Nn." "Nhn." "N." "Nn."
"Nhhn."
"Nnnhn." Nn." "N." "Ng." "Ngg." "Nn." "Ng." "Nng." "Nng." "Nng." "Nng." "Nng." "Nng."

47

"Nng." "Nng." "Nng." "Nng." "Nng." "Nng." "Nng." "Nng." "Nng." "Nng." "Nng." "Nng."
"Nng." "Nng." "Nng." "Nng." "Nng." "Nng." "N." "Nng." "Nng." "Nng." "Nng." "Nng." "Nng."
"Nng." "Nng." "Nng." "Nhng." "Nng." "Nng." "Nng." "Nng." "Nng." "Nng." "Nng." "Nng."
"Nng." "Nng." "Nng." "Nng." "Nng." "Nhng." "Nng." "Nng." "Nng." "Nng." "Nng." "Nng."
"Nng." "Nng." "Nng." "Ng." "Nng." "Ng."
"Nnn." "Nn." "Nnnh." "N." "Nhn." "Nh." "Nh." "N." "Nh." Nhn." "N." "N." "N." "N." "N." "N."
"Nhn." "Nhn." Nh." "N." Nhn." "N." "Nhn." "Nhh." "Nh." "Nhn." "N." "Nnn." "Nng." "Nn."
"Nn." "Nn." "Nnhn." "Nn." "Nnn." "Njn." "Nn." "Nnhn." "Nnnhe." "Nnh." "Nn." "Ng." "Nn."
"Nnn." "Nnnnn." "Nnm." "Nnmn." "Nnm." "Nm." "Nmm." "Nmmn." "Nmbm." "Nmbm."
"Nmbmv." "Nmnb." "Nmbnb." "Nmb." "Nvnmb." "Nmvnb." "Nb." "Nn." "Nn." "Nnn." "Nmn."
"Njn." "Nn." "Nnn." "Nbn." "Nnk." "Nnlmn." "Nn." "Nnm." "Nnnnn." "Nn." "Nnknln." "Nnb."
"Nnnn." "Nnnnnb." "Nnnnbnm." "Nnnnb." "Nnnbhn." "Nnnnbmhb." "Nbmn." "Nnbn."
"Nbnbmn." "Nbnbmbn." "Nnnb." "Nnn." "Nneme." "Nnne." "Nnnmene." "Nnmne." "Nnmnemn."
"Nnnmng." "Nnnmng." "Nnnb." "Nmnn." "Nnnv." "Nnnnm." "Nnnmn." "Nnne." "Nnnn." "Nn." "Nn."
"Nn." "Nnnn." "Nnnn." "Nn." "Nn." "Nn." "Nnmn." "Nhn." "Nhhn." "Nnhn." "Nnh." "Nnhnb." "Nbnnh."
"Nnhn." "Nbgb." "Nnhn." "Nnhne." "Nnne." "Nnne." "Ne." "Ne." "Ne." "Ne." "Ne." "Ne." "Neh." "Ne." "Ne."
"Ne." "Nenhe." "Nen." "Nenh." "Nnenh." "Ne." "Ne." "Ne." "Ne." "Ne." "Ne." "Nne." "Nne." "Nne." "Nnh."
"Nnr."
"Y." "Yh." "Yhh." "Yhn." "Ynh." "Nhn." "Nh."

"Nntr." "Nntr." "Nntr." "Nntre." "Nhtr." "Nnh." "Nnt."
"Ner." "Ntnre." "Nnty." "Ntey." "Nnt."
"Nte." "Nte." "Nten." "Netn." "Net." "Nten." "Nnte."
"Nn." "Netn." "Nnte." "Nnte." "Nten."
"Ntn." "Nent." "Nte." "Net." "Netn." "Nnt." "Ngeng."
"Ng." "Neng." "Ngn." "Negn." "Nhe."
"Nnret." "Nen." "Nne." "Net." "Nr." "Nr." "Nt." "Nrth."
"Nn." "Nneng." "Nnee." "Nen." "Nen."
"Nrn." "Nrne." "Nne." "Nny." "Ntny." "Ntyr." "Nry." "Nt."
"Nrty." "Ntr." "Ny." "Ntry." "Nyr."
"Nty." "Nyo." "Nrt." "Nrh." "Nrnh." "Nnr." "Nnr." "Nrn."
"Nnr." "Nhnr." "Nhrn." "Nrhn." "Nrh."
"Nr." "Nnr." "Nr." "Nnhr." "Nnh." "Nnh." "Nhn." "Nh."
"Nnh." "Nrhn." "Nrh." "Nnhr." "Nhnr."
"Nnrh." "Nhnt." "N." "Nht." "N." "Nh." "Nh." "Nnh."
"Nh." "Nn." "Nhn." "N." "Nhn." "Nt."
"Nhn." "Nh." "Ntn." "Nt." "Nhn." "Ntn." "Nh." "Ndnt."
"Nnth." "Ntn." "Ntn." "Nt." "N." "Ntn."
"Nnt." "Nd." "Nn." "Nt." "Ntn." "Ndtn." "Nt." "Ndt."
"Ndtn." "Nt." "Ntn." "N." "Nn." "Nnn."
"Nn." "Nt." "Nt." "Nn." "N." "Nn." "Nnn." "Nt." "Ntn."
"Ntntn." "Ntt." "Nt." "Nnt." "Ntn."
"Ntn." "Ntehm." "Ntehn." "Ntm." "Nt." "Nmnt." "Nm."
"Nmm." "Nm." "Ntm." "Ntnm." "Nntn."
"Nhn." "Nte." "Netn." "Net." "Nrgb." "Ntg." "Nunm."
"Negnm." "Neh." "Nhg." "Nn." "Nnh."
"Nnh." "Nre." "Nnrh." "Nnghr." "Nnh." "Nnn." "Nnht."
"Nh." "Nhnht." "Ng." "Nge." "Nlt."
"Nte." "Ntbg." "N.t" "Nh." "N." "Nn." "Nnth." "Nt." "N."
"Nn." "Ntn." "Nhnt." "Nnt." "Nnt."
"Nte." "Ntn." "Ntn." "Nen."
"Nten." "Nh." "Nn." "Nhnh." "Nn." "Nh." "Nhnnh."
"Nhne." "Nen." "Nt." "Nnh." "Nhn." "Nn."
"Nhn." "Nn." "Nnh." "Nhn." "Nt." "Nhn." "Nn." "Nhn."
"Nen." "Nhen." "Nenh." "Nh." "Nnh."

Nhn

"Nth." "Nthn." "Ne." "Nen." "Nt." "Ntne." "Nen." "Nen." "Nh." "Nen." "Nh." "Nne." "Nth."

"Ntn." "Ntnh." "Nn." "Nnn." "Nnhhen." "Nhn." "Nhn." "Nn." "Nnnh." "Nnhn." "Nhnhne." "Nn." "Nne." "Nhn." "Nhn." "Ntn." "Ntn." "Nt." "Nn." "Nt." "Ntn." "Ntn." "Nen." "Nne." "Nen."

"Nhehn." "Ne." "Nfh." "Ntn." "Ntnf." "Ne." "Ntn." "Ne." "Nen." "Ntn." "Nh." "Nthen." "Nnth."

"Nn." "Nh." "Nnhe." "Nh." "Nhn." "Nn." "Nhtn." "Nh." "Nhn." "Net." "Nt." "Ntn." "Netn."

"Nte." "Ntn." "Nen." "Nnth." "Nn." "N." "Nh." "Nnht." "Nh." "Ne." "Nh." "Nnh." "Nhn."

"Nhnhn." "Nh." "Nn." "Nt." "Nhn." "Nh." "Nhn." "Nth." "Nnht." "Nh." "Nhn." "Ntnh." "Ne."

"Nn." "Nt." "Nh." "Nhn." "Nhn." "Nth." "Nhm." "Nwn." "Nw." "New." "Nw." "Nw." "Ne." "Wn."

"Nhh." "N." "Nnwrnn." "Nnw." "Nhr." "Nhr." "Nwrhn." "Nw." "Nwn." Nhwn." "Nhnwr."

"Nnwh." "Nwnh." "Nwrh." "Lnwr." "Nnw." "Nnwr." "Nwn." "N." "Nn." "Nnr." "Nwnt." "Nwnt."

"Nrn." "Nn." "Nntrw." "Nn." "Nr." "Nn." "Nnrt." "Nn." "Nw." "Nr." "Nn." "Nn." "Nnrn."

"Ntnrw." "Nwn." "Nnw." "Nnw." "Nntnh." "Nymte." "Neea." "Ne." "Nhe." "Net." "Ne." "Nre."

"Nw." "Nttb." "Nw." "Nw." "Nbw." "Ng." "N." "Nw." "N." "Ne." "N." "Ne." "Nde." "Nhe." "Nefn." "Ng." "Nen." "Nsn." "Ns." "Nhhne." "Nwhwr."

"Nhrww." "Nw." "Nwnn." "Nv." "Nn." "Nnnhn." "Nwnh." "Nth." "Nn." "Nw." "Nw." "Nw."

"Nwe." "Ne." "N." "Nw." "Ne." "Nf." "Nwe." "Nfwe." "Nw." "Nfe." "Nw." "Nfe." "Nnne."

"Ngrnhn." "Ner." "N." "Nn." "Nn." "Nnn." "Nn." "Nn." "Nn." "Nn." "Nn." "Nar." "Nar." "Nnr."

"Na." "Na." "Nr." "Nn." "N." "Nn." "Nnn." "Nn." "Nnr." "Nhw." "Nn." "Nnw." "Nn." "Nwr."

"Nn." "Nnrw." "Nn." "Nw." "Nnrwhn." "N." "Nnrwn." "Nrw." "Nw." "New." "Nwer." "Nr." "Ne." "Nr." "Nn." "Nn." "Nwe" "Nh." "Nteh." "Nth." "Ne." "Nh." "Njn." "N." "Nth." "Neh."
"Nyr" "Ny." "Nsry." "Nry." "Ny." "Nn." "Nn." "Nne." "Nen." "Nn." "Ne." "Nne." "Nen." "Ne."
"Nny." "Nn." "Ny." "Nny." "Nee." "Nen." "Nn." "Nnhnn." "Nnh." "Nneh." "Nn." "Nen." "Ney."
"Neny." "Neoy." "Nyoe." "Nyoe." "Nnoye." "Nyenh." "Nesth." "Nsen." "Ne." "N." "Nn." "Nn."
"N." "Nne." "Ne." "Ne." "Nhne." "Ne." "Neln." "Nen." "Nenht." "Nhye." "Nen." "Ney."
"Ne.""Nn." "Nn." "Nn." "Nnnn." "Nhth." "Nhy." "Nn." "Nhy." "Ng." "Nyl." "Nh." "Nyh." "Ny."
"Nny." "Ny." "Nyh." "Nhy." "Nn." "Ny." "N." "Nhn." "Nn." "Nhn." "Nyh." "Nyh." "Nhyn."
"Nhy." "Nnn." "Nyn." "Nyr." "Nyehr." "Nyrn." "Ny." "Nnyee." "Nhhuy." "Nny." "Nr." "Nnr."
"Ny." "Nyn." "Nry." "Nny." "Nrn." "Nn." "Nhy." "Nwh." "Nrt." "Nh." "Nhr." "Nt." "Nrh." "Ne."
"Nh." "Nr." "Nnnh." "Nb." "Nnhy." "Nhn." "Ny." "Ng." "Nye." "Nn." "Nn." "Nhn." "N." "Nne."
"Nn."
"N." "Nnnnnnn." "Nn." "Nnn." "Nnnnh." "Nnnhen." "Nhh." "Nne." "Nhn." "Nehn." "Ntehn."
"Nhn." "Nn." "Nh." "Nhn." "Nnh." "Nn." "Nh." "Nnh." "Nh." "Nn." "Nnn." "Nhn." "Nn."
"Nhnn." "Nn." "Nnh." "Nhnt." "Nthnn." "Nth." "Ngh." "N." "Nh." "Nnh." "Nh." "Nn." "Nht."
"Nht." "Nt." "Nnh." "Nn." "Nn." "Nnn." "Nn." "Nh." "Nn." "Nnn." "Nhn." "N." "Nnn." "Nn."
"Nn." "Ne." "Nhnhe." "Nne." "N." "Nen." "Ne." "Ny." "Nen." "Ny." "Nen." "Nn." "Nnnn." "Nhn." "Nhn." "Nn." Ng." "Nn." "Nng." "Nng."
"Nn." "Nng." "Nnh." "Nng." "Ng." "Nn." "Ng." "Ngh."

Nhn 51

"Ngh." "Nh." "N." "Nn." "N." "N." "Nn."
"Nng." "Nn." "Nnnn." ".Ngn." "Ngn." "Ng." "Ng." "Nh."
"Nn." "Ng." "Nng." "Nh." "Nn." "Ng."
"Hn." "Nn." "Gn!" "Ns." "Ngn." "Nn." "Nr." "Nr." "Nn."
"Nrn." "Nnnr." "Nr." "Nn." "Nh." "Nn."
"Nh." "Nn." "Nhn." "Nn." "Ng." "Ngn." "Nh." "Nng."
"Nnng." "Nn." "Ng." "Nr." "Nh." "Nn."
"Nn." "Nh." "Nn." "Nn." "Nh." "Nnh." "Nm." "Nh."
"Nhm." "Nn." "N." "Nn." "Nn." "Nnm."
"Nh." "Nehneh." "Nnh." "Nm." "Ngn." "Nh." "Nn." "Nh."
"Nm." "Nmmmnh." "Nm." "Nh."
"Nh." "Nn." "Nmn." "Nnn." "Nnn." "Nnmn." "Nnm."
"Nnh." "Nhn." "Nhn." "Nm." "N." "Nn."
"Nmn." "Nmnhhe." "Nnh." "Ngh." "Nn." "Nh." "Nmnn."
"Nh." "Ng." "Nh." "Nn." "Nn." "Nh."
"Nh." "Nnh." "Ng." "Nh." "Nn." "Nn." "N." "Nnn." "N."
"N." "Nhn." "Nhne." "Ng." "Nhg."
"Nn." "N." "N." "N." "N." "N." "N." "N." "N." "N." "N."
"N." "N." "N." "N." "N." "N." "N."
"N." "N." "N." "Nn." "N." "N." "Nh." "Nh." "N." "N." "N."
"N." "N." "N." "N." "N." "N." "N."
"N." "N." "N." "N." "N." "N." "N." "N." "N." "N." "N."
"N." "N." "N." "N." "Nn." "N." "N."
"N." "N." "N." "N." "N." "N." "N." "N." "N." "N." "N."
"N." "N." "N." "N." "N." "N." "Nh."
"N." "N." "N." "N." "N." "N." "N." "Nh." "N." "N." "N."
"N." "N." "N." "N." "N." "N." "N." N."
"N." "N." "N." "N." "N." "N." "N." "N." "N." "N." "N."
"N." "N." "N." "N." "N." "N." "N." "N."
"N." "N." "N." "N." "N." "N." "N." "N." "N." "Nn." "Nhn."
"Nhne." "N." "N." "N." "N." "N."
"N." "N." "N." "N." "N." "N." "N." "N." "N." "N." "N."
"N." "N." "N." "N." "N." "N." "N." "N."
"N." "N." "N." "N." "N." "N." "N." "N." "N." "N." "N."
"N." "N." "N." "N." "N." "N." "N." "N."

"N." "N." "Ng." "N." "N." "N." "Hn." "N." "N." "N." "N."
"N." "N." "N." "N." "N." "N." "N."
"N." "N." "N." "N." "N." "N." "N." "N." "No." "N." "H."
"N." "N." "N." "N." "N." "N." "N."
"N." "N." "N." "N." "N." "N." "N." "N." "N." "Ne." "N."
"N." "Ln." "N." "N." "N." "N." "N."
"N." "N." "N." "N." "N." "N." "N." "N." "N." "N." "N."
"N." "N." "N." "N." "N." "N." "N." "N."
"N." "N." "N." "Hn." "N." "H." "N."

Anger is just sadness turned inside out

Tim Etchells

A duo of two idiots get a job to murder someone who owes money (in large quantity) to a self-styled badass in the psycho geographical low parts known mainly as Endland (sic). When people say that guy's name aloud (i.e. name of the Badass) they take their eyes down to the dirty ground where all the chewing gum and other stuff is stuck on it or else look off into the distance out of camera shot, well away to the place where the various bridges, schools, hospitals and other organs of the state are being knocked down. Anyway. The recently hired idiots put on black clothes they believe suitable for murder and also gloves that absolve them of fingerprints and balaclavas so that no one will be able to recognise them. They pick up a heavily discounted axe at a hardware store and pay for it, then pick up a large length of wood that is leaning against the wall of a nearby building that they think they will use as a partially improvised club. Then they go round to the guys house and knock on the door or ring the bell repeatedly but all the same; no answer. Shit says one of them - murder is easy enough, that is the easy part, an

idiot can do it, any idiot, but you cannot murder someone if you cannot locate them. That is one of the problems of our chosen professional (sic), says the other; the best hired assassin in Old Rome or London Town still has to track down or otherwise locate his victim and an idiotic double act like us has to do just the same.

Waiting, they sit in their car opposite (a red Peugeot Anodyne) and smoke some spliff trying to get calm and listening radio. One of them is one kind of character and the other is another kind of character, at least that is what they pretend. One pretending to be quiet and silent strong type and the other pretending to be friendly rapscallion and spilling over in full-tilt joy of life, full of weakling talk and anecdote. The time he went to Marbella and got paid to get laid, the time he got trapped in a toilet cubicle that turned out to be a difficult one to get out of, the time he stole a grandfather clock by hiding it in a coffin, the time he squandered his brother's winnings on a misplaced lottery ticket but bought him a pair of unwanted cuff-links in a gesture of unexpected compensation, the time he volunteered for a medical test and was given a bogus placebo and so on ad infinitum. It would have been tedious even if they weren't stoned, it was above, said his more silent-like superior sidekick, it was above and fucking beyond.

When the guy came back home they clubbed him from behind on the driveway, cut him down to the gravel like a dead tree or like a bag of frozen potatoes, then used the axe to hack him up to a smaller size just small enough to fit in the boot of the car without having to fold him.

*

They drove their car to find the badass boss guy who for reasons no one really understood still worked as a night security guard at a deep-freeze food warehouse called Tundra. There he was, dozing in front of his many screens, watching channels of nothingness, zoned out, the Facebook opened on his laptop computer, the TV on in his background playing One Million Mega Babes or re-runs of Laughable Planet.

One of the idiot assassins rapped his knuckles on the window and the Badass gestured irritably to the door. Then in a exaggerated slow-motional pantomime of human communication the idiots gestured with thumbs, eyes and hands that Badass should come outside cos they had got something to show him and Badass motioned in response with fingers and eyebrows to say "bring it here if you got something to show me."

There was a pause and an amount of exasperated eye contact.

Then the chief idiot called the badass on his mobile and said "look you have to come look outside—you do not want me to bring this thing that I have got out here into your place of workship."

"Place of work," the badass said. "It is not a place of workship—you are thinking of a place of worship."

"That is what I am saying," replied the idiot, "I do not want to bring it in your place of Workship—you have to come outside."

The whole conversation was just proof of how

complicated things were in Endland before the days of complete Computerisation of everything. And it was slow too as was often the way of such things. Up on the dirty wall the clock switched to slow time, the seconds inching at a decelerated pace that would have certainly raised an eyebrow at CERN, the minute hands hesitating and lagging and dragging as though made apparently of a kind of sentient lead.

Once they got Badass out in the car park the idiots proudly popped the trunk to their car to show off the corpse of the bad debtor bloke they had previously chopped down to size and bundled up inside there.

"Jesus Christ on a Motorbike," said Badass, staring into the fetid darkness of the trunk. "I can't make head nor tail of this. Where is his face?"

"There," said one of the idiots with a confidence that was rapidly contradicted by his colleague saying "No, that is his foot."

"This is not the right bloke anyway," said the Badass after pause of several human seconds. "This is not Gilligan. This is not the fool that owes me millions."

"Who is it then?" asked one of the idiots but by that time Badass was already walking back to his portacabin. "I do not know and I do not care," he said over one of his shoulders.

"But…"

"Don't 'but' me," said Badass, "You've produced a

narrative anomaly. An orphan event. An irrelevance."

"Shit," said one of the idiots, calling after the Badass but still looking down into the trunk. "It's a corpse. What are we going to do with it?"

"I do not care. That is your problem idiots. You have killed the wrong guy."

*

Whether it was some unfortunate error of Google maps or a human map-reader error, or an understandable error of communication or a slip of the tongue or a typographical error or just one of those things that happens sometimes in Endland no one could say for sure and anyway each idiot secretly blamed the other, each suspecting that his colleague was in fact the true idiot of the team and cause of all malfunctions.

In silence and without really thinking they drove the car to the top floor of a car park in the edge of the town, a familiar place on top of a hill where as younger idiots they had sometimes bought drugs or else brought mentally defective girlfriends to make love in a car or where on more Lonely Nites© they had thrown stones at pigeons or listened in to private conversations belonging to other people using a kind of hand-made radio scanner. For them it was a home of sorts; a multi-storey sanctuary, a charmed hiding place, far above the town.

"We have killed a man," said one as they sat there rolling another spliff.

"It's not the first time," said the other, "remember that guy we killed in Doncaster. Or that one we killed in Kurdistan. He made a terrible sound and we faced a prosecution for noise pollution."

"Yes. I remember." Lighting the spliff and affecting the wide-eyed and far away look he had seen sometimes on YouTube, "Of course I remember. That was different tho. That fool had it coming. This guy we killed last night was all like Mistaken Identity, an Innocent Man. With kids or hobbies or . . . Shit. It is just like Badass said, he has no place in the narrative. We have to get rid of him, otherwise the structure will not Hold."

The second idiot was not a complete expert in narrative theory and started a confused jabbering speculation about sub-plots and U-turns and revelations but every time he went back to look in the boot at the sad tangle of dead flesh, mortality stench, and bloody clothing he had to admit that they were in trouble.

As night turned to early morning the view from the carpark went from deep black to a strange shade of violet caused in part by the dawn and in part by local damage to the upper levels of the atmosphere in terms of Toxic Emissions. The two of them were looking out at the city, shifting their gaze from the former Steel Works to the brand new TimeWarnerG4S Detention Centre and conversation turned again and again to possible routes for disposal of the body.

They had no time for the meat grinder and chemicals route and anyhow knew from too many movies that that shit left residue, which could also damage narrative integrity. They discussed the wasteland/bin-bags option,

Anger is just sadness turned inside out

the sack-binding-rocks and canal possibilities, the shallow grave deal and even the improvised funeral pyre/human arson solution favoured by some of the more enthusiastic drug gangs locally. But nothing seemed right. It was all too difficult, too final, too much to get their pathetic stoner heads around.

The talkative idiot kicked off on a long more or less free associative trail; talking about something his brother once said, about an incident he'd once been involved in during a war in Afghanistan, about a girl he fancied that turned out to be a guy, about a horse he backed in a horse race that had stumbled and died, about drugs he had taken, believing them to be some new kind of Ecstasy but how they were really some kind of Despair. I cannot go back there he said, I cannot go down there, I cannot go back down. It wasn't clear if he was talking about the place he had got to, the drugs he had taken or about a well which had climbed inside during an incident in his childhood. Then he started to cry, freaking out completely like the mad guy in *Crazy Heart*.

That was when the not-so-talkative idiot slapped him, inducing silence and turned off the radio also, with its promised "endless hard-beat of heart-beats and heartaches." ©

And it was then, also, as the poets say, that the not-so-talkative idiot opened the car door with Resolve. "Get out," he said, "we are going. Get out. Stop crying. This is it. We are leaving."

"What?" said his compatriot. "What?"

"We are going."

"But..."

"Do not 'but' me. We are just going to lock the car and walk away. We can leave this dead guy here. He's an unwanted corpse. We do not need to take responsibility or face impact of this in our lives."

"But..." The talkative idiot was more or less panicking.

"We lock the doors and walk away, we never come back here, we never speak of what happened. This narrative branch can sort itself out. Or it's a dead end. It does not matter. It is not our problem, whatever Badass says. We look after our own endings, this dead guy can fend for himself and what happens next."

With that the two of them were already walking away from the car to the malfunctioning elevator, climbing in it and starting their descent, not bothering to look at the dirty human handprints or read the graffiti that said ANGER IS JUST SADNESS TURNED INSIDE OUT and RAW FUTURE NOW. They were talking, breathing steady. Descending. And walking away. Moving forwards. Moving on out. As they went out the doors and down the steps to street level they were still talking, already riffing on things that had happened, about a film they once saw with a science fiction flavour, set in Rotherham but filmed in Spain. They were talking above love and about holidays, about things they wanted for their kids. About sanity and options. About money. About sex. And at the top of the building, locked tight and silent in the boot of the Peugeot Anodyne the dead man waited his slow time in the dark void of the trunk, waiting with no will to anything, no will to story, but still potential for it. An anomaly or orphan event. A left-over. Yes. Or a closed

door that might also be an opening. An end that might or might not be the beginning of something else.

Sheffield. 2013.

When Attitudes Become Form*

Johannes Fa

Side by side, their faces blurred,
The artist and curator lie in stone,
Their proper habits vaguely shown
As well-cut Armani, stiffened pleat,
And that faint hint of the absurd -
The little dogs under their feet.

Such plainness of the post-post-modern
Hardly involves the eye, until
It meets his left-hand white glove, still
Clasped empty in the other; and
One sees, with a sharp tender shock,
His hand withdrawn, holding his hand.

They would not think to lie so long.
Such faithfulness in effigy
Was just a detail friends would see:
A sculptor's sweet commissioned grace
Thrown off in helping to prolong
The Latin names around the base.

They would no guess how early in
Their supine stationary voyage
The air would change to soundless damage,
Turn the old tenantry away;
How soon succeeding eyes begin
To look, not read. Rigidly they

Persisted, linked, through lengths and breadths
Of time. Snow fell, undated. Light
Each summer thronged the grass. A bright
Litter of birdcalls strewed the same
Bone-littered ground. And up the paths
The endless altered people came,

Washing at their identity.
Now, helpless in the hollow of
An uncurated age, a trough
Of smoke in slow suspended skeins
Above their scrap of history,
Only an attitude remains.

* This text is a version of Philip Larkin's "An Arundel Tomb" (1964) from *The Whitsun Weddings* published by Faber & Faber (2001 edition).

Dear Paul, Francesco and Alex

Melissa Gordon

Dear Paul, Francesco and Alex,

I apologize for being so late with my response to your publication, I fear I've delayed things way beyond the normal length of permissible time and an excuse or at least an explanation is due to you.

I'm not normally late with things, or would like to think I am not tardy, generally bad with time or at worst seemingly lazy or, perhaps even worse as an artist: disorganized. In my head I think I come across as a responsible person, someone who delivers the goods, in the right place, at the right time. Pertinent. Attentive. Efficient.

Having said this, I seem to be writing, "I'm sorry I haven't gotten back to you sooner," in so much correspondence recently, and wonder if this in itself points to a problem—is there a need for an apology to not respond immediately? Isn't responding immediately a way to get a conversation out of the drafts folder, and so the act of taking time becomes a sign that the gravity

of the situation is fully taken in before a slight and compromised response is churned out? The other side of the coin could be: thoughtful, considerate, responsive.

I don't know which side of the coin I'm on, any of the time. But each side poses maybe two halves of a question that is driving me to distraction: what is it that is the root of trust in the character of the artist, and what is it about trust that is at the root of value in the art environment?

Maybe a good place to start is with first impressions, which are all about context. Location historically in art was about proximity, and art history is taught in this causal manner: something literally rubbed against something that rubbed against something else. At the basis of this 'timeline' of art history is peer groups-collectives and initiatives, which many women have pointed out seem to have double the amount of members in black and white photos than in the catalogues that house them. But how do you trust an artwork at first glance? Can one have faith in an unknown object in an unknown context? Language itself gives no clues, whether something is naïve, cynical, shocking, tentative: these all describe values of both positive and negative inclination. As you approach the cliff edge of a work itself, what can you hang on to?

Nothing. And so what is required is the next heading in my gathering set of notes with no conclusion: a leap of faith. This sounds so heavy, I'm wary to say it. But I feel that underneath the act that is the most basic necessity in seeing art—giving it a chance—lies a constantly shifting set of concerns or criteria that are absolutely to do with a set of beliefs that are delivered—whether via a communal decision making process or an overt

construction of power structures is not to be decided in this letter, certainly, but needs be put into context. How do we 'read' a piece within the context of a practice, an exhibition, an environment? What happens when something is recognizably 'sensitive' or 'flitting'—can it be appreciated as being such, or must it be understood within a larger context of unexpected relationships to such subject matter? If a man and a woman each take a picture of flowers, whose is more critical, automatically? And what of the reversed situation, who is more flippant about a sculpture of heavy stature? Is it a distinction of expecting certain contexts to be subjective and others objective?

I don't know if talking about criticality without exemplifying it in any way shape or form is, well, setting a bad example for flabby artist writing. But there's something about the word critical that strikes a teethy nerve, because it has inherently mutable value. To critique something is different than just straight up 'being critical'—or embodying criticality. To 'be' critical, I have to be trusted to do so—and where can this possibly come from? I've seen people attempt to belittle others, interrupting, talking louder, faster, walking away, and I've seen talks that outline endless research, but neither constitute an embodied (embedded?) criticality in work which can be supported by all the language in the world but has to physically enact whatever it's intentions are. It's got to Do it.

How to Do it? How do expectations get fulfilled? They don't really, in art, ever. Are we all performing our subjective critical spheres—and are our characters at the forefront of these little performances? I hope not, I have an inherently faint heart at the word 'subjective'—its

basis being a 'subject,' such as: what is the subject of my enquiries as an artist? Surely whatever it is it is wider than my sphere, my city, my friends. Surely it is not about whether you like it or not, or even if you understand it.

Which leads me to my final conundrum, a final illustration of the damned-if-you-do and damned-if-you-don't situation which I find myself thinking about, whether or not I can relate to it, which is the question of the role of seduction within the sphere of making and presenting works. Who wants and who gives? It seems like a cyclical dynamic which is about sex, basically. How can you be seductive without being a tease or give it up without being a whore? How crude. Pardon my language. In the relationship of the viewer and the maker, it's often the maker wanting the viewer, or seducing the viewer, even though it is exactly the opposite that is the POV of the art historic trajectory: the artist, not looking at the camera, he stomps on the grass, he moves around… :

> *I enjoy working on a large canvas. I feel more at home, more at ease in a big area. Having the canvas on the floor, I feel nearer, more a part of the painting, this way I can walk around it, work from all four sides, and be in the painting. Similar to the Indian sandpainters of the West. Sometimes I use a brush but often prefer using a stick, sometimes I pour the paint straight out of the can. I like to use a liquid, dripping paint. I also use sand, broken glass, pebbles, string, nails or other foreign matter, A method of painting is natural growth out of a need.*
>
> *I want to express my feelings rather than illustrate them. Technique is just a means of arriving at a statement. When I am painting I have a general*

notion as to what I am about. I can control the flow of the paint. There is no accident. In that there is no beginning and there is no end. Sometimes I lose the painting. *

---

* Jackson Pollock, transcribed from *Jackson Pollock: '51*, directed by Hans Namuth (1951).

Tails

Alex Graves

There was a muted, but unmistakable, note of anxiety in the voice of the black-suited man in the back of the taxi as he asked the driver how long it would take to reach the airport.

The taxi driver grinned at him in the rear-view mirror, a strip of brown skin and merry eyes.

"About twenty minutes sir. Don't worry, you won't miss your flight."

The man in the suit nodded and began to slide a laptop in a black neoprene sleeve out of his shoulderbag. The driver glanced at the mirror again.

"Where are you flying to sir? If you don't mind me asking."

The man in the back answered with a single word.

"Very good sir. Very good. And will you visit the hanging gardens? I am told they are very beautiful."

On hearing that his passenger would not visit the city at all, that he would not leave the hotel near the airport in which his meeting was being held, and that, if he could please be excused, he had a lot of work to get on with, the taxi driver grinned again.

"That is a very great shame sir. To fly all that way and not visit the hanging gardens. A very great shame."

The taxi sped past industrial buildings and chain-link fences in the early morning sunshine.

~

In the vast arrivals hall of the airport the man in the suit—one of many—searched for his check-in desk. He had donned a pair of rimless spectacles. A small trolleybag rolled behind him.

"Hello Mr–"

The check-in girl, who may have been pretty beneath her mask of makeup, carefully enunciated the surname on the passport she had been handed.

"May I see your carry-on bags please."

He pointed to his shoulderbag and his trolleybag on the floor: two xylophone notes tapped on the air. She nodded and began to type, glancing from his face to the angled screen on her desk, as she recited a list of questions.

"Did you pack your bags yourself sir?"

"Are you carrying any prohibited items sir? Any firearms,

explosives, aerosols, poisons, blades?"

"Did anyone put anything in your bag or tamper with your luggage in any way?"

"Did anyone ask you to carry anything for them?"

The hall was full of confused sound: announcements, conversations, beeping luggage carts, babies crying, automatic doors swishing open and shut.

"Enjoy your flight sir."

He strode away before she could finish her salutation. An involuntary impulse made her raise her voice slightly, trying to reach him.

~

"Got a laptop in there sir?" asked the heavy woman in the blue security uniform.

She was looking at the queue behind him as she said, "Take it out and place it in a separate tray."

The man in the suit lined up two of the grey plastic trays on the conveyer belt for the X-ray machine. He put his jacket, along with the contents of his pockets—phone, keys, wallet, a few loose coins—in one of them. Then he took out his laptop in its black sleeve and laid that in the other. As the belt dragged the trays towards the X-ray machine and its curtain of dangling rubber strips, he added his trolleybag and his half-empty shoulderbag to the monotonous procession.

The alarm honked as he walked through the square arch of the security gate. He had forgotten to remove his belt. A male security guard holding a black plastic wand gestured him to one side. The guard—who smelled at close quarters of cigarettes—ordered him to stand with his arms raised and ran the wand down his thighs, over his buttocks, up his flanks.

Close by, a woman was being similarly scanned by a female guard.

~

Waiting in the queue for a coffee shop, the man in the suit took his phone from his pocket and began to stroke, tap and flick the screen. The queue shuffled forwards, bearing him with it. He continued to frown over the glowing screen.

"What can I get you sir?"

The small, dark woman behind the counter had been joking with her colleagues in a foreign language. As she interrupted the suited man's concentration, her voice, and her slightly lopsided smile, still brimmed with foreign laughter.

He paused for a long time—pulling himself out of his phone—then ordered an espresso macchiato.

The odour of grinding coffee was both sickly and enticing.

~

"Passport and boarding card please."

The phrase, repeated with slight variations, was murmured alternately by the two officials manning the desk at the entrance to the departure gate. The passengers heard faint echoes, soft transmutations, of their own instructions as they pocketed their documents and took their seats in the gate.

The man in the suit handed over his passport with the boarding card closed inside it. The bored expression of the official—a very young man, almost a boy—did not alter as he examined the sullen photograph giggling with holographic colours, the beetle-like microchip trapped inside the laminated paper. He placed the passport face down on a scanner built into the desk. A fringe of white light showed around the cover of the small red book.

Behind the desk, through the tinted glass of the airport walls, a jet rose slowly into the bright morning sky.

~

On the bus to the runway he stood with one hand looped inside an overhead strap, his trolleybag cradled between his feet. He was pressed now and then against the soft body of an obese man. The man—also in a suit, with a sharply trimmed goatee that did not quite succeed in delineating his jaw—made an apologetic face at their first contact; after that he pretended not to notice.

Someone had the volume turned up on their headphones. A ghost of music haunted the bus, tinny and cold.

~

He moved slowly along the narrow aisle of the aeroplane, frustrated by people removing their jackets or hoisting bags into the overhead compartments. When he came to his row—thirty six—a bald man in the aisle seat flapped away his newspaper and allowed him to edge past. A woman of about sixty arrived soon after. She glanced several times from her boarding card to the number above the row before claiming the window seat.

~

As soon as the seatbelt light went out, he reached down between his feet for his shoulderbag. Moving carefully—to avoid touching his neighbours' legs—he withdrew his laptop and opened it on the fold-down plastic tray. Almost immediately he began to type. Alerted by the cockroach scurry of keys, the woman in the window seat turned to look at the man beside her. She vaguely recognised the pattern on his screen: the fronds of multicoloured text with their undulating line of indentation, the alien poetry of fused words, underscores, braces, brackets and dots. She had seen it over shoulders before. Her gaze moved up to his face, lingered for a moment, then returned to the toy city receding beneath the window.

The bald man took out a thick book of Sudoku puzzles and laid it on his tray.

~

An air steward came by, dispensing drinks from a

trolley a few centimetres narrower than the aisle. His cleanshaven smile roved over row 36, H-K: the lady peacefully asleep by the window, the two men lost in a laptop and a book.

"Would you like a drink sir?" he asked.

The bald man's pen paused in its smooth, apparently random trajectory, filling box after box with neatly-formed digits. He asked for a glass of tomato juice.

"Something to drink sir?"

The steward knew before he spoke that the man in the suit would not look up from his computer. His smile moved to the row behind.

Pale sunlight spread from the curved windows and overlapped across the cabin.

~

Emerging from a cushioned avalanche of sleep, the woman in the window seat was surprised to see a mountain range—bare of clouds or snow—unscrolling beneath the plane. She watched the unknown land for a while through a thinning mental fog; then she reached for the novel that had lain in her lap since the flight began. Before she started reading she looked once more at the man beside her. This time it was not his typing, but rather its abrupt cessation, that caught her attention. She wondered what could have derailed his train-like industry. She did not expect him to be staring at her. Her gaze remained fixed—barring those tiny, seemingly instantaneous, rotations with which the human eye

unravels its surroundings—as the fine muscles of her face began to perform a symphony of feeling. In the first movement her eyebrows lifted, gathering above them the soft, wrinkled skin of her brow; and her other features slid up the same bright scale, eyes widening, lips almost parting as her jaw slackened behind them. The second movement swapped the sharp allegro of surprise for the grey andante of confusion. Her eyes retightened, crinkling slightly at the corners, while the furrows on her forehead shifted inwards and the lines around her mouth were drawn to a worried, quizzical purse. In the third movement the most strident notes of the second—anxiety and sorrow—were singled out and intensified. Her frown deepened, the darting of her pupils accelerated, her lips began to waver with unvoiced words. The crescendo grew until her blinking eyes—dull with age—were glossed by a thin, incredible sheen. At last it was broken by the percussive clash that marked the start of the fourth and final movement: her gaze dropped to the mesh pouch of pamphlets and magazines on the seatback. As her head turned slowly back to her book, the music of her muscles was a diminuendo of dissonant themes: pity, embarrassment, disbelief, sadness, solicitude, paralysis and fear.

The bald man—who was wearing a shirt tucked into a pair of blue jeans—waited patiently in the aisle for his smartly-dressed neighbour to extricate himself from the seats.

~

The smiling steward returned, holding a green refuse bag.

"Any rubbish to collect? Any bottles, wrappers, empty cups?"

The bald man handed over a plastic cup with some napkins and wrappers wadded inside it. The woman by the window started from her novel as if a balloon had just popped. She began a flustered collection of the detritus of the short flight: a half-full bag of mini pretzels, a few sweet wrappers, an empty plastic water bottle. She fumbled the bottle into the vacant chair beside her. When she tried to recover it she dropped it again, this time down the front of the seats. The bald man smiled genially at her and leaned over to fetch the bottle. As he was passing it to the steward, it slipped from his hand and he trapped it between his thighs.

"Must be catching," he said, beginning to laugh, "if you'll excuse the pun." The woman shook her head and managed to smile.

He handed the bottle to the steward who promptly missed the mouth of the green bag and had to bend down to retrieve it. Both passengers laughed and the woman clapped once as the steward thrust the bottle into the bag, saying, "Thank God that's over!"

~

Fifteen minutes before the flight was due to land it was brought to a flight attendant's attention that one of the bathrooms was still occupied.

Passengers twisted in their seats, straining against their seatbelts, for a view of the commotion at the rear of the plane. Between the backs of the flight attendants and the

woman who had responded to the call for a doctor, they caught glimpses of a supine man in a black suit. They learned more, however, from the unguarded expression of one of the stewardesses hurrying down the aisle.

As the plane continued its smooth descent, two attendants kept up an exhausting rhythm of compressing the dead man's chest thirty times with the heels of their hands, then breathing twice into his open mouth with his nose pinched shut.

White noise blanketed the cabin, just as it had since the plane took off. It was as if the flight were accompanied by an orchestra that could only play a single note—every note at once.

Cody Foster

Bruce Hainley

made his hardcore debut
in *Malibu Pool Boys*,
a famous flip-flop scene
with swarthy Chad Knight
you could call jaw-dropping.

Born Shawn Louis Sumner,
on October 9, 1970,
he died,
in Grand Junction, Colorado,
on January 7, 2007,
apparently of liver cancer.
Thirty-seven's about the right age to.

He fostered the early '90s "California chic" aesthetic
—summed up summer,
sun-tweaked shag,
jock's tan bod,
gaze usually untroubled
by thought,
existence untroubled
by much more than a jockstrap—
a look

it would be difficult to prove
ever really goes out of style,
not to mention determining when
exactly it hasn't been in.

Rough trade was his genre.
A tawny, unforgettable, streetsmart bottom,
at a time when muscle usually only topped,
he was not uncut or unhung;
his asshole's lightly furred.

He owned 1992.
Fucked nonstop.
Coined new entries on definitions
of the word *brawn*.

Three years later
—troubles slurred over as
"run-ins with the law"—
he "disappeared,"
not long after starring in *Workin' Stiff*
as a bootblack.

Whatever it's called,
life, love or its lack,
incarceration,
he endured.
What most consider his "return,"
despite a few scenes in the early "aughts,"
Foster delivered
a year before his death
in *Tough-Man Bondage*:
he hangs from all fours, piñata,
while some brute works up a sweat,
whipping and spanking his ass;

he whines, pleads, begs, screams and shudders,
"better than anyone else in porn," a fan claimed.
I'm not sure what that means
but feel I've been there certain times.

In the sort of online obits
that post such stats,
before the listing of his height ("5 ft 8 in"),
weight ("180 lb"),
eye color ("blue"),
hair color ("blond"),
and ethnicity ("American")
was his dick size ("7.5 inches").

His life, like others', was turbulent, infirm.
Here lies one whose fame was writ in sperm.

Moda:WK

Nadia Hebson

I'm here in the middle distance, mid-career, teaching job, childless by choice, in the studio figuring out what painting could be. Way out on the periphery, you may not know my practice but you may recognise me: unusual clothes, subdued colours, men's shoes. I always give that same rejoinder about the shoes. If you move in teaching circles we might have met, you usually say "Who are you?" puzzled I am not on your radar, quickly followed by, "Where have you come from?" I will give you the Berlin narrative and you are invariably satisfied.

None of these details matter, they are coordinates that may or may not explain this connection, real or otherwise to Winifred Knights (1899-1947).

Look at the photograph.
Studio 6, British School at Rome 1921.
As AR remarked when I described the image to her, there's something important about seeing another woman in the studio. She described "the shudder." Implicit understanding that we didn't underscore… thank fuck.

"...I've stood on the highest balcony of Villa Medici in the small hours and at some point later in the day momentarily glanced at Antonella da Messina's 'Youth' and whilst the pairing of a grey linen skirt with a discrete cambric blouse makes perfect sense to me, the painting remains unfinished..."

I know that portrait of a youth, I had a copy with me. Why? Clear faced, quiet tension, a rim of linen against a fleshy neck: skin, tears, curls against sweaty foreheads, grey marl, dead black, laid light, every inch desire. You know I know precise northern European paintings are not about the narrative.

Rome, were you in a state of perpetual excitement? Nineteen, exemplar of maturity and discretion, your guardians named it, *The Deluge* repeats it, slattern grey, geometric forms drag the eye from left to right. Complex-continental modernism, meets an unrepentant British figuration. The world is tilting. A dull light catches a series of flat dead planes, the eye scans back across the immersion. Near silent. Figures step into their own shadows.

Is the background the past, seemingly exhausted and the foreground this precise moment?

I now know that that is you standing right of centre, self-portrait in a grey dirndl, or are they culottes? A plain centre parting, hair fixed in a coiled bun at the nape of your neck, faintly austere I thought at first. I misunderstood. Make sense of the details. Scanning the photograph of you and Barbara Hepworth at leisure in the cortile, she is yet to form, a slight figure blinking in the Roman sun, clothed in gauzy Edwardian shift,

the conservatism of youth. You have broken free, complex like the painting, eluding categorisation. Your correspondence reads as if things make perfect sense; paintings do not take five years to complete. The ridiculousness of picture making? The Impossibility of Painting? Anxiety versus self-belief. (Too clever or not stupid enough to be just a long-game painter?) I need to tell you the other resident artists (all men, all mediocrities) need to be kept at bay.

The 22nd March, 1922. You describe a humorous incident that occurs near the Spanish Steps two weeks previously. Two young men accost you, both painters; you must surely be an artist's model, those extraordinary clothes. In six languages they persist. Grey green convent coat, black stand collar, drawn at the neck, breast and hips, three neat rows of ebony buttons, sleeves taut to the wrist, from hips to calf, a perfect bell of worsted fabric. Charcoal "picture hat," high heels and a ferruled cane. The get up is audacious. With a grin you reply when would you have time to sit you are an artist in your own right. Not to reduce you to a tableaux of outfits against an early 20th century backdrop. But I do you a disservice if I skim over this as some inconsequence, those daily acts of toilette, the precise designing and fabricating of the clothes, or are they costumes? This careful, measuring of a persona. Your modest thrill at your headway in the world, a patient receiver of persistent compliments, that consistently misunderstand and misrecognise the quarter you hold (your depth, your seriousness, your facility, perfectly sentient—all spelled out in the paintings) These things: jackets, bust bodices, shirts, stockings, hats, are and are not just clothes to you but no-one around you can take this thought, this possibility any further. I surprise myself when I name

this as your life's real misfortune; from here it casts a
long shadow.

The scenario at the Spanish Steps is not a solitary
incident, your correspondence and the recollections of
those who knew you name many more. Harlequinade,
dancing in the library, standing naked in your studio
in front of the borrowed mirror. An improbable thing,
self-styled, here and then gone. At that moment beyond
comprehension, beyond your own comprehension.
Quietly announcing your presence in the world through
a series of complex but discrete actions. Cutting a dash
that focuses attention and garners respect; an intelligent
move, conscious or not.

From 1921-25 all constituents are in balance: self-belief,
facility, sense, health and the attention of others. Your
strength as a painter is to coolly meld your own narrative
into taut, distilled scenes. Levelheaded and precise,
somehow this is a compliment. Yes, Spencer, a hint of
De Chirico, but above all Piero, whose women manage to
out-maneuver the one dimension. How apt. Present in all
your paintings (and a great deal of your contemporaries)
you are the axis from which the tone proceeds.

The Marriage at Cana
Space marked and truncated by precise geometric forms,
terracotta foreground flat to the eye limned with shifting
black diagonal (irrigation ditch). Outside under dense
ilex an austere meal takes place. Women, men, seated in
squared opposition. Coral pink ellipses pattern across a
blue linen tablecloth. Distilled narrative sense where the
least important element is the story. Look to the right,
not the left. Branch coral necklace traces the nape of a
neck, hand rests on the tables edge, table rests on the

terracotta floor, floor bisected both in the foreground and left hand mid-ground by disturbed aqueous line. Tension forms in the conversation, the forms in conversation, the smell of last night. Index finger, loose in your hairline recalls the tear of the zip, the zip's snag of your hair.

In the architecture of the paintings there are gaps, physical, where one world ends and another begins. Sometimes bridged and sometimes not, by hovering forms that cast a direct shadow onto the ground below. Two feelings are irreconcilable. Formal devices reduce the world to planes of complimentary colours: rust finds its opposite in a peerless sapphire, aubergine skirts a slub grey. Tone to emotion as mute bone walls catch the last light of the evening sun.

Elements of the paintings become irresolvable. Bare linen and reverse silhouettes mark this shift in psychology. I need to tell you this device makes perfect sense. A metered image complete from seam to seam is a thin excuse. As dull as pewter.

Fiona Jardine

my effects

Was she a ghost? Then?
Everything was new that day.
She turned. A shadow fell through her.
Even then, was she a ghost?

We were adrenalised, slightly at odds with each other.
I was comfortable in exile because I felt sure I was received
through my accent. It didn't matter that often, it was
misplaced – Australian, Kiwi, South African, Irish. Welsh,
even. I could go to one of those ex-Pat pubs
and take a welcome.
For sure, I wasn't English. I enjoyed my little bit of
marginality.

The geometry that pins her in place, to the steps of that
concrete library, has its origin in me. I hold on to her.
I keep her fixed.
And I see her, across the expanse of a paved quadrangle, a
remote skirted figure, hurried, turning against the last rays of
the sun sinking somewhere behind me.

On route, we saw your father take off into one of those ex-Pat
pubs, a paper folded under his arm.
Just the edge of your father we saw, at the threshold of one of
those ex-Pat pubs. It's name, The Adam & Eve.
Just in time, he turned in.
That paper, An Poblacht.

The square was familiar you. At this exact stop, daily, you
would descend from the top deck
and swing onto the pavement.
The scene acquired volume as a measure of your habit,
the same in sleet and spring, the same
on days in-between.

You know, on a trip, it is easy to see signs.
A long black hair snaked down a sink,
like the course of the Thames past Richmond. The indelible
stain spreading from a pen in your pocket.

When we saw her, I thought she was a portent.
For me. For us. For my time away.
But she was a portent unto herself, turning in the last shaft
of light. For that moment,
vectors put in motion something that came to resolution in the impression of her skirted figure.
Yet, for weeks and years, she was nothing but a coincidence.

Linden green, I feel, you noticed. The first flush of tender,
translucent leaves, a corona diffusing.
We swung off the bus in a chemical burst.
Everything was new.
Thixotropic, an aura seeping from the West
across these streets.
Turning, she squints against the long angle of the sun.
The shadow that falls through her is mine.

I hesitated it seems. Poised to register her turning, I thought,
to look at the clock. Supposing the vagary of her gait, in a
blink, London bluffs position her once and for all on the
library steps.
That night sucked into the subway,
fully charged,
scattering drinkers before us.

Like a pebble, that scene for you.
The size of something to turn in your hand.
Ballast in your pocket.
And in my effects.
No photo.

even then

Morning Verses, 22/09/12

Allison Katz

<u>Verse</u>
I am not a practical person.
Practicum.
Practice.
Every morning I wake up,
the world is new to me,
again.

<u>Verse</u>
The first regret
is having to write it down.

<u>Verse</u>
(He was, by the way, the kind of man who

<u>Verse</u>
Wrong, but it happened anyway.

<u>Verse</u>
3 weeks in
we change the plan
made a month ago.

<u>Verse</u>
He treats me like his mother
He takes my abuse

<u>Verse</u>
In the garden
they procured forgetfulness

<u>Verse</u>
For dinner,
he made
her swear never to again.

<u>Verse</u>
The Thames starts moving.
Someone in Oxford is running a bath.

<u>Verse</u>
The helicopter, the clear sky.

<u>Verse</u>
The Sun that has no precedent.

This is a Portrait of You If I Say So

Valentinas Klimasâuskas

Dear Reader,
This Is a Portrait of You If I Say So

Your distrust regarding this kind of portraiture is understandable. Your reaction very much resembles that of Iris Clert the moment she received the telegram: "This is a portrait of Iris Clert if I say so. Robert Rauschenberg." [i] The telegram was disposed, but later it was salvaged from the garbage by Iris—slightly crumpled —and put on display.

Has the telegram become a self-portrait as Iris was crumpling the text into a 3D structure, into her self-portrait, and a monument of portrait genre at the same time? Most probably not, especially if you are able to destroy the symbolical of the text, the text as the portrait, thus, uncovering self-portrait of both. By misidentifying the telegram as just a telegram and not as her own portrait Iris misidentified her own portrait as the representation of herself. Later on, when she recognised the crumpled telegram in the recycle bin (or in her memory, perhaps) as the representation of her,

this was not the portrait Rauschenberg intended: his portrait of Iris was symbolically destroyed by crumpling, by recycling. It could also be that Iris has not recognised herself in any of the portraits and that she perceived the telegram to be an artwork.

All messages in the telegram, of the telegram, as the telegram, have changed.

The performative statement "This is a portrait of you if I say so" is as legitimate as Friedrich Nietzsche's "Every name in history is I," when I is the link between both statements and you is exactly the I that you have in mind.

Valentinas Klimasâuskas

---

[i] In 1961, American artist Robert Rauschenberg (1925-2008) was invited to participate in the exhibition at the Galerie Iris Clert, where artists were to create and display a portrait of the gallery owner Iris Clert. Rauschenberg's submission consisted of a telegram sent to the gallery declaring "This is a portrait of Iris Clert if I say so."

If you don't identify this portrait with "a portrait of you" and you are about to tear off and throw away this page, you may first like to refer to the instruction piece *Untitled* (1995/96)* by a Swiss-American artist Christian Marclay (b. 1955):

> Tear out this page while listening attentively listen and crumple the page into a small ball you can repeat these sounds with other pages save the ball(s) discard the book.

* Christian Marclay's *Untitled* appears in the DO IT archive on e-flux website: www.e-flux.com/projects/do_it/homepage/do_it_home.html

Have you ever slapped a dead person?

Shana Lutker

Surrealism + corpse.
This equation first brings to mind the psychoanalytically endowed (and occasionally exquisite) exquisite corpses, and the game that produces them. The exquisite corpse now resides comfortably in popular culture. But the Surrealists left two other corpses behind—traitorous, tormented corpses who lie deep in the belly of the French National Library—*Un Cadavre* (1924) and *Un Cadavre* (1930).

The two *Un Cadavres* are also Surrealist in character— they exemplify their abrasive, cantankerous side, mobilized through printed pamphlets and editorials, they struck out against other literary and artistic personas that challenged or threatened their Surrealist projects. Now yellowed and brittle, showing their age, both *Cadavres* are 4-page broadsides printed in Paris between the wars. The first *Cadavre* was distributed on October 18, 1924. The second on January 15, 1930. The first *Cadavre*, whose subject was Anatole France, was released 6 days after the French poet's death. It was written during the last

weeks of his life; as the citizens awaited the news with the doctor's bedside reports, and the Surrealists took to their typewriters. The second *Cadavre*, whose subject was André Breton, was released 36 years, 8 months, and 16 days before the French poet's actual death. Both were written while their subjects were still breathing.

The two *Cadavres* were intended to offend, to anger the lovers and followers of the (purportedly) deceased. In the case of Anatole France, the newspaper claimed that though he had just died, he would never die, we would never be able to get rid of him. In the second *Cadavre* decidedly more cruel, the body under attack was living, was the primary instigator of the first *Un Cadavre*, and as Breton was the self-appointed but widely accepted founder and leader of the Surrealists, the paper amounted to a mutiny.

+++

Today it reads as rather tame, but the first *Cadavre* was, in its time, supremely shocking—people were outraged. To attack Anatole France, literary icon, just days after his death was desecration. (The surrealist's wanted the paper to come out on the day of his death but the nervous printer held it back almost a week.) To be clear, the Dadaists-turned-Surrealists never liked Anatole France. This was not a mentor who had disappointed them—this was a beloved writer accepted by both left and right, a Nobel laureate, who placated everyone and embodied everything the Surrealists despised about French literature. France's people, though probably familiar with nonsensical Dadaist antics, were not pre-conditioned for the invective of the new upstart Surrealists.
The release of *Un Cadavre* precedes the first Surrealist

Manifesto by a week or two. The Manifesto was on the press as *Un Cadavre* went into distribution. And so this was the beginning of Surrealism, in it's most proper sense. The movement that began in opposition to Dada in 1922, was now speaking for the first time in a collective voice, literally defining it's terms. Hans Richter, Dadaist and historian, wrote, in *Dada: Art and anti-art*, "The word Surrealism, invented by Apollinaire, was first of all used as a weapon to destroy Dada. When Breton states that he was a Surrealist even when he was a Dadaist, this is perfectly true, as far as he personally is concerned. His right to the work 'Surrealism' was disputed at first by Paul Dermée and Ivan Goll, who had started another kind of Surrealism, but with Breton's first *Surrealist Manifesto* (1924), signed by all those who until a short time before had been Dadaists, such questions were finally settled." Sort of.

For reference, here is the definition of "Surrealism" articulated by Breton in that first *Surrealist Manifesto*:

> SURREALISM, n. Psychic automatism in its pure state, by which one proposes to express—verbally, by means of the written word, or in any other manner—the actual functioning of thought. Dictated by the thought, in the absence of any control exercised by reason, exempt from any aesthetic or moral concern.

> ENCYCLOPEDIA. *Philosophy*. Surrealism is based on the belief in the superior reality of certain forms of previously neglected associations, in the omnipotence of dream, in the disinterested play of thought. It tends to ruin once and for all all other psychic mechanisms and to substitute itself for

them in solving all the principal problems of life.
The following have performed acts of ABSOLUTE
SURREALISM: Messrs. Aragon, Baron, Boiffard,
Breton, Carrive, Crevel, Delteil, Desnos, Eluard,
Gérard, Limbour, Malkine, Morise, Naville, Noll,
Péret, Picon, Soupault, Vitrac. *Un Cadavre* doesn't
seem to embody any of these directives exactly,
except, perhaps in the way it seemed to express that
which was not Surrealist, namely, Anatole France.
One could surmise that they had an idea and once
it was hatched, they did moved forward "in the
absence of any control exercised by reason."

My French is rather terrible, but here I wrangle a
translation of Breton's contribution to *Un Cadavre*(1924):

REFUSAL OF BURIAL
If, when he was alive, it was already too late to
speak of Anatole France, let us resign ourselves
to cast a glance of recognition on the journals
that prevail, the wicked newspapers that brought
the news. Loti, Barres, France, a beautiful white
sign marks the three sleeping friends: the idiot,
a traitor and policeman. I do not object to the
third, a word of particular contempt. With France,
it's a bit of human servility that leaves the world.
Whether celebrating the day we buried cunning,
traditionalism, patriotism, opportunism, skepticism,
realism or lack of heart! Consider that the most
vile actors of that time took Anatole France as an
accomplice but never pardoned him for waving
the colors of the Revolution while smiling inertly.
To bury his corpse, someone on the banks should
empty a box of these old books "of the beloved"
and put him in it and throw everything to into the

Seine. It takes more than death to turn this human into dust. -André Breton

The other "articles," by Philippe Soupault, Paul Éluard, Pierre Drieu La Rochelle, Joseph Delteil, and Louis Aragon, are also attacks on Anatole France that take on the literary world and those who blindly revere Anatole France. His writing, according to the Surrealists, was boring, derivative, patriotic crap.

On the same day that *Un Cadavre* was released, a letter from the Surrealists was published in *Le Journal littéraire*. This letter, translated below, reveals the Surrealists themselves in the role of policemen, playing bad cop to Anatole's good cop, perhaps:

> To Pierre Morhange, 50, rue de Douai, Paris (9th).
> Paris, October 11, 1924.
>
> Sir,
> We warn you once and for all that if you permit yourself to write the word "Surrealism" spontaneously and without notifying us, we will be a little more than fifteen to correct you with cruelty. We don't want to have to tell you again!
> Bureau for Surrealist Research
> Signed: Paul Eluard, Louis Aragon, André Breton, Roger Vitrac, etc.
> (*Le Journal littéraire*, October 18, 1924.)

The *Un Cadavre* broadsheet ends with a bold declaration, in all caps, "*A LA PROCHAINE OCCASION IL Y AURA UN NOUVEAU CADAVRE.*" [Next time, there will be a new body.] This implies the Surrealists intended to decry other corpses. Ultimately, there would be just one

additional cadaver.

+++

When hell freezes over, when pigs fly, when chicken have teeth—only then, we imagine, would Breton himself imagine that he would be the second corpse of the Surrealists.

As the premier *Un Cadavre* was followed swiftly by the first manifesto of surrealism, the second *Un Cadavre* came just weeks after the second. *The Second Manifesto of Surrealism* was published on December 15, 1929, in the twelfth and final edition of *La Révolution surrealiste*. This second manifesto, according to Breton's biographer Mark Polizzotti, was unquestionably "the angriest and most bitter of Breton's major works."

One month later, the second *Cadavre* is a direct response to the manifesto. It's front-page prominently displays a large image of the then 33-year-old Breton's head encircled by a crown of thorns, and begins with a quote pulled from the first:

> Il ne faut plus que mort cet home fasse de la poussiere. -André Breton (*Un Cadavre*, 1924)

Translation: "It takes more than death to turn this human into dust." (Or, perhaps, "It will take more than death to turn this man to dust.") The contributors to this *Corpse* were ten recent-ex-Surrealists; Georges Ribemont-Dessaignes, Jacques Prevert, Raymond Queneau, Roger Vitrac, Michel Leiris, Georges Limbour, J.A. Boiffard, Robert Desnos, Max Morise, and Jacques Baron; plus Georges Bataille and Alejo Carpentier.

In this 1930 edition, Breton's public and private personas are torn apart. Leiris accuses Breton of being a corpse who thrives on other corpses (of Vaché, Rigaut, and Nadja), and more than one brought up Breton's overly sensitive nature ("over a line in the newspaper, he kept to his room for eight days, and spat, spat everywhere... he spat on the dinner that was not ready on time, he flew into a rage at a sardine can..." wrote Prévert in "The death of a man.") The attackers knew their enemy, and knew that this was a man who could dish it out but couldn't take it.

Today, this second *Un Cadavre* still comes across as terribly mean! Five-hundred copies were printed and sold on the streets to baffled and confused passersby. Outside of the Surrealist bubble, neither side of this war of words seemed very rightgeous.

When the paper reached Breton, he was devastated. He fell into a deep depression. He didn't leave the house for weeks. And his "obituarians" didn't let the cadaver lie, they kept at it; they prank-called his house in the middle of the night, they sent him funeral wreaths. The attacks went on and on. His lover Suzanne once again left him and moved out of the apartment, made anxious by the barrage. Breton became rather obsessed with the idea that a collective suicide was the best way out of the Surrealist experiment.

Of course, not everyone turned on Breton. Shut-in at his house on rue Fontaine, he received letters of support, even from strangers. Yves Tanguy, housemate of Jacques Prévert, ended their longtime friendship in protest of Prévert's participation. Even *Paris-midi*, a newspaper known for its' ridicule of the Surrealists,

printed a note about Breton's "woeful mistreatment." Paul Eluard swore he'd make things right. Poor Breton. Yes, he was the behind the first *Cadavre*. Yes, Breton attacked innumerable former comrades and colleagues in despicable and childish ways. Yes, he had declared himself the leader of the Surrealists, and certainly, his reign must some day come to an end. But is the only way to kill Breton, the pope of Surrealism with an overdose, to keep kicking the corpse when he's already on the ground?

All Prices
Are Delayed

Nicholas Matranga

Nothing more direct than an exclamation mark. And it was just that as the one yelled at the other. The body language was immediate and spoke loudly to the situation. Never mind the facial expression since it was merely a tool to get the point across.

Two strangers have just met on the street. Do they recognise each other? No, they are strangers. And it just happens that they are walking into the same restaurant and are very much in the same mood. Maybe that is the reason they seem to have such familiar faces? They both sit down at the counter, finding each other separated by an empty swivel chair. Two coins fall from the pocket of the waitress. Nervously she jingles the coins in her palm as she walks across the restaurant to the kitchen.

Annoyed, a man shouts, "I ordered these eggs scrambled! You fool."

Having finished his late lunch, a meaty cheeseburger, the man stands up from his swivel chair, thinking…

The waitress runs after him explaining that he has forgotten his change. The amount left appears to be too much for a gratuity. The man turns, looks, and smiles as the doorway moves past him.

Meanwhile, he is late for an appointment.
"Time to run."

Back at the counter the other man is joined by someone he really does know. They shake hands, neither with an expression of friendship. The handshake is firm. The two men say things like, "Can you believe that trade?" and "Would you mind relaxing it with your leg?" Perhaps shaky leg syndrome, "I have never seen anything like it."

The waitress comes by and I smile.

The two men stand, shaking hands and take turns tripping over one another. One stands slightly higher than the other; however this is corrected by the shorter man consciously adjusting his posture. Very straight. They turn towards the door.

"Are you the type of person to slap a friend on the back as a sign of camaraderie?"

Children have a tendency to play with their food. Even liquids. I have never found pleasure in having liquid in my nose. My mother would condemn such behaviour, "Please don't snort."

The booths of the restaurant are uneven and lumpy, giving everyone back-pain. Half the tables stretch like synchronised swimmers before a competition. If you don't believe me you will just have to take my word.

I pull my neck up as far as I can bear and feeling my vertebrae, they spread to the point where the upper two might just pop. This makes me blink.

At my table I have the company of my dentist, who happens to also be a close friend, he reminds me not to order cake or a milkshake, as I have an appointment next week. He also complains of a patient whom he refers to as a chronic tooth grinder. What a pain it is that he is a dentist and I think, "If only he had become a vet he could neuter my cat at half the price."

I had fancied chicken and have it in front of me. It is rather dry. MMMM, his beef smells delightful! I think my chicken may have sat for most of his life on his back and that might be the reason it is so tough to chew. Or the cook is to blame. I consider a visit to the kitchen.

A woman from the booth behind ours taps me on the shoulder inquiring if she might have our table salt. I hand it to her without a thought.

My friend lifts his hand into the air in a shy manner trying to get the waitress's attention. He says: "How about I get this one and you can take me for soup after our next appointment?" Swiftly I think, hmm-mm, and nod, "That would be just fine with me." What does he know about the soup?
"Hey, what do you think about leaving?"
The restaurant is all but empty. For the most part we are the last patrons. "Yes!" Grabbing our belongings.
"Don't forget that."
"Ah, yes, thanks!"
We get up and walk stride for stride to the door; one holding it open for the other.

"That's it, I guess I will see you soon?"
"Without a doubt."

Looking out to the street and not looking where I am going, I trip and nearly fall on a loose paving stone. What are the chances? A few steps behind me is my friend, standing there with his Blackberry, delicately typing away about a canine that might need to be pulled this evening.

I now walk along the pavement putting together in my mind the last remaining priorities of the day. I guess I should think about buying some groceries sooner or later. I said I would. Just up the next block and to the right is a rather nice delicatessen. I will have a look.

Nearing the window I notice the employees beginning their preparations to leave for the day. They are cleaning the machinery of the shop and wrapping the cheeses and meats. I ask myself, "Should I bother them?"

bone (cadaver)

Katrina Palmer

The leash, short and leather, linked the dog and its owner. Fastened loops at each end were drawn taught around the throat of the brutalised animal, frenzied and pulling against its constraint at one extremity while at the other the loop cut across and around the owner's fist, progressively tightening. The sight of this disturbed her as much as his booming voice filling the room, telling her to get up from behind the desk and say something, as if she could have. Her words were thrust back down her throat by his bellicose performance. She sat silent and transfixed by the deranged dog, until he kicked it hard in the ribs. That's when she stood up and heard her own voice saying, "Let it go!" He stopped shouting and allowed his hand to release its grip—a controlled gesture with a slow mean ease, in downright contrast to the hell-for-leather leash that whipped past and vanished from his palm, indeterminately.

    The dog ran and jumped at her throat, knocking her from her feet. Impressive canines pierced the exposed skin of her neck. The owner backed out the door, attempted to appeal to the dumb creature but exited with his commands contracted and pointless because the dog

had other ideas. Ferocious jaws penetrated down into her trachea, split the esophagus and ripped out her pulsing jugular.

At the very top of her vertebral column there was a string of bones—they interlocked to create an articulated attachment with her skull. The dog tore these bones from her body. He carried them out of the room, and away—over fences and across alleyways until he reached a distant mud-filled garden. In the far corner, behind a dry tree stump, he kicked back dirt to form a hole in which he buried the bones.

Unbound from his tyrannous owner, and with the slack leash still around his neck, he exercised his freedom to dig the bones up again and to spend time developing an attachment to them. There were seven ring-like cervical vertebrae for him to play with—each individual bone was comprised of a series of convex and concave surfaces, extended lips, lateral masses and a central cavity.

One of the bones was especially compelling—the atlas above the axis on which the head turned. This was the uppermost bone of her vertebral column and it was a grave and beautiful object. It had the widest most generous aperture making it nothing more than an ivory ring around a hollow opening. The dog loved that about it. And subjected to his protracted attention it soon separated from the rest of the string. He pushed his tongue around its contours, slobbering and sniffing, sensing this bone was in some way very special, although he could not appreciate that such a peculiarly empty object once formed a crucial link that connected her spine to her skull.

He buried the bone again only to dig it up, to lick and chew on it, to suck and rebury it. Every time he secured the precious bone in the ground, out of sight,

he could not settle until he reassured himself that it was still there. Every time he rediscovered it, infused with the scent of his affections, the sensual complexity of his treasure reaffirmed his instinct to indulge his desire. But the dog's repeated action was compulsion rather than choice. He buried his bone only to dig it up again and again.

CRAB MEAT

Siôn Parkinson

This is a story about evisceration, and about seeing things with one's own eyes. Yet it is also about (around and above) the point at which clinical detachment meets familial intimacy. As the 17th Century English physician, William Harvey, who reputedly dissected both his dead father and sister, might have argued, this kind of detachment is necessary for objectively observing the living and the dead, whether brothers, sisters, fathers, family pets—or crabs.

The characters and their names overlay historical fiction and autobiography. Those characters more discernible to the reader (though chronologically muddled and fictionalised to hell) would be John Hunter (1728-1793), Scottish surgeon and younger brother to William Hunter (1718-1783), Scottish anatomist and physician, respectively our ROBERT and JOHN-JOHN.

First performed with projected image, soundtrack, and additional electronic voices at Limoncello Gallery, London, 5th September, 2012.

ROBERT –

"EXPERIENCE IS EVERYTHING," I'll say,
later and often, but we must begin
mustn't we? with the imagination.
Imagine. Experiment. Observe, yes?

---

*Specifics: The last words of this story—
that is, a story in parts about parts;
images described in aerial view—
the last words of this story are* CRAB MEAT.
*The beat, ten syllables a line, is set
by the tap-tapping of a cat and dog
who share the name, Harvey, and whose forepaws
stretch through space and time as if glistening probes;
like beasts with multidirectional limbs.*

Perhaps there is nothing in EDNA's hand
when, this morning, JOHN-JOHN climbs from the coach.
Instead, she smiles, truly pleased to see him
and hopeful, too, for what he might now bring.
Or does she know what he has done before—
will do again when our sister worsens,
coughs and expires with an arm in the fire?
Or maybe there is   in her hand
                (there is!)
a round stone the size of a strawberry,
or possibly a piece of pottery—
a piece of pottery with broken point
poking between her fingers in a fist?

———————————————————————

What can I tell you about my brother?
A man with some work. A man of something.
A man who returns four days in receipt
of a letter by mother, imploring:
"can be done?" "beg," "return at earliest."
And more: "she's in wont of your," etcetera.
With his tools and a bucketful of crabs,
our eldest living brother will race home.

Specifics: My face. This relentless mouth
looks as if it were cut for me with shears.
A reddish down is starting to appear
on my lip, and prescient of the beard
I'll grow later in life, for which my wife
will most cruelly admonish me for.
It will come between us, this face and hair,
both figuratively and literally.
She'll rebuke my kisses on inner thighs,
saying it is not lips she feels but bristles,
like a something-or-other, scuttering.
Maybe it is, I'll say. Maybe my beard
hides within it an undernourished mouse,
a small army of butterfly larvae
so that I might conceal their hairy backs,
releasing them in stealth and saliva
and out my mouth just to titillate her.
And for months, maybe, I'll cling all the more
to the red hair on my cheeks and my chin
and, too, to cries of my being uncouth.
"If the sight of my jaw or lip," I'll say,
"is enough to shake men from their pillars—
or a wife from her pillow, for all that—
what will they make of the spur out my cock?"

Here we project close-up a cockerel's head,
a crescent moon sprouting forth from its comb.

He puts the bucket down between our feet
speaking of how he'd come by the creatures,
how he'd doubted their fitness for the pot:
"in their instar phase of moulting," he says,
though what he really means is "between shells."
He says that as they travelled on the road,
and with the carriage rocking back and forth,
he could hear the animals' insides slosh.
This occasions a joke about my brains—
"hydrocepha-something-or-other," and
the consequences of my truanting.
"Well, why not make your own schooling?" he says,
kicking the pail in loud punctuation
and tendering its live contents to me.

Specifics: My eldest living brother:
My mother and father's first born son, John,
died aged fifteen from falling off a horse.
(Father would die in a similar way
though mad drunk and out the door of a coach.
THE BIG MAN's brains were such soup from the fall
there was no hope of rising from the slab
in the kind of weird reprieve one might read
in books that later collated such tales.
Yet for THE BIG MAN there was no such luck.
No way: he was pâté. Brown meat. Fish bait.)
So, when the second Hunter son was born
he was given another brother's name.
To his elder sisters, and later, me,
he became, thus, a double John: JOHN-JOHN.

Later, will JOHN-JOHN not admit us all
into that Autumn-cooled chamber, with breath
stinking of spirit wine and black pepper,
and ANNIE, naked, laid out on the oak,
already tracing the wood grain with nerves?
Will he not permit us, despite our pleas,
to see her in this last remaining hour?
"It's too something," and "risk of contagion,"
he'll say, wiping a hand down his britches.
Well, we know, don't we? "Like he did Father."
Honest to God. He anatomised him.
Or, as he said, "made a preparation."
Better still, "a conjuration of light."
And it must have seemed so, there on his bench,
a square of Isobella sun cast on
the freshly varnished flesh of our father
layered up, coat on coat, till he glistered
like a tallboy set for elytrous flight—
Like the sea-smoothed hull of a ship, he shone.
I wonder, had he muttered to himself?
Bearing blade and brush, muttered to himself,
indemnifying with words: "Meat, crabmeat,
pig bladder, candy apple," etcetera.
A few hundred years from now

                             (the future!)

in the anatomical museum,
the University of Edinburgh,
when you see THE BIG MAN under perspex
and inside, a blue cotton bed-sheet, draped:
"a bad choice surely," and "shows up every,"
you'll say, pointing to bits of skin and hair—
likely an eyelid that's come unstuck when
moved from one display case to another.
"Did you see the Gaffer tape?" you'll whisper.

What am I saying, O, relentless mouth?
And what do I mean, "O," instead of "Ah"?

The crab is still alive and drums the ground
with its tapering limbs in a ten-beat.
This part is hard for me to speak about,
knowing what I know from way, way up here,
and seeing all eventualities
in the present tense, stretching out round me
like – yes! I can see it all perfectly–
a beast with multidirectional limbs.
For example, I know that at this point,
here, with HARVEY, my wolfdog, beside me,
in a corner of the yard, or outhouse,
I know that I have never before seen
any living thing such as this: a crab.
Perhaps a pig kidney fried with carrots;
hands trapped, writhing under a pink boulder;
Mother in aprons, crimping a pie crust–
images I see now like plates in books,
but never have I seen one in the flesh.
So, as we look down now, from up above
as if hanging from wires round our ankles,
and the crab in the centre of the cloth,
(Superman's S-shield stretched across the earth)
we see that for an eleven-year-old
and a younger brother who does-not-know,
I move with alien dexterity.
Still, it seems to me, readying my tools,
that this is all so unfamiliar.
At what point, I will forever wonder,
at what point does one ever truly know?

Siôn Parkinson

Harvey raises a paw and taps the earth.

___

At what point does he know, for that matter?
For example, if I satisfy him
and offer up the crab to his pink grin...
Ho! See, he yelps as it pinches his ear!
He knows that! Pain. Un-anaesthetised. True.
But wait, look here: the whole arm detaches,
and even still the creature's claw clings on.
For a short time, the two animal-parts
are locked in a heroic episode
of impossible microgravity.
And as arm and ear are wrestling nearby,
the crab's body, as if in slow-motion,
falls to earth, landing miraculously
back into the centre of the sackcloth.
"It's both here and there," I say to myself
before pulling off its remaining limbs,
arranging them with tensors still twitching.
Oily bubbles appear out its mouthparts
before a bilious liquid spurts forth.

___

Specifics: The reason for the sloshing.
It's core, ill-fitted to its carapace,
is like a shrunken moulage; an offprint;
a child with developing dentition;
like a son in his fathers shirt and shoes.
(As JOHN-JOHN says, "between shells," remember?)
Thus, a superfluity of wetness.

I'll speed up, for there is too much to tell.
Beneath the biscuit of shell I've removed
is the body, alike nothing we've seen,
all undifferentiated tissue—
an accretion of colourful jellies
weeping into one another like goo.
Harvey is back sans claw, and taps the earth,
but not before he blocks our view to lick
the still pulsing box-heart of the creature.
It's now we get a sense of symmetry,
a sense of structure and segmentation,
plumes of filaments and deadmen's fingers
and thumbs peeling back vitreous membranes,
moving through lusters of purple and white,
probing cavities and snipping cartilage
and antennae; eyestalks from their orbits.
Disentangling vessels with fingernails
and weighing in palms what might be organs,
(it all goes in the mouth and warms like spice!)
until we are almost at the sackcloth

and HARVEY still tap-tap-tapping throughout...

---

as I raise and rotate the semi-shell
to peel down its apron: "We have a girl!"
At the centre of its pennant, a hole,
a hole that leads to the heart, and to light.

All at once, we are moved ahead in time,
a few hundred years into the future.
A newspaper spread out in double sheets.
A kitchen table. An operation.
In triangular configuration
there is a man sat with his young daughter
plus a cat the colour of white Pepper

---

who raises its paw and taps the table

---

pressing for some meat amassing in bowls.
THE BIG MAN is mistaken in thinking
the cat knows how to beg, let alone count.
"Do you see?" he says. "Do you see? He taps!"
Yes, even a cat can be taught to tap
if its stomach burns with expectancy.
"It's an exercise in patience," he says,
but, and the cat knows this, as does the girl,
it's the levy of fear over impulse

that halts a mad dash over the table.
Back of the hand, maybe, but more likely
the heavy handled knife, held by the blade,
and forming such a devastating priest,
(and yet allowing for such precision!).
"You ever bitten down and gotten shell?
Sends a shock, I'll tell you. Stops everything."
Like a peeping eye spotted through the chink.
"Some good preparations, and it's a breeze."

From here, there's little left to pick over.
Some closing dialogue, hard to make out:
"you do is," "now listen, I'm showing you,"
"gently," and "what you do is, now gently!"
"you strike it," "you hit it," etcetera,
"in the palm of your hand, and tap." "here, here,"
"don't," "no, no, not like that," "gently, I said."
"the trick is," "now the trick," "the trick here is,"
"like this," "the best bit," "you save that for your,"
something, and "push with your," "and then forwards,"
and "don't tear," "now you're not," "your finger there,"
and "there! That time." "Do you see now? He taps!"

The odor girding our scenes is replete.
It is everything. The whole ball of wax.
Salt caramel and rabbit viscera.
It's the air. Or, if the air were to smell,
not the blue specks of vaporised matter
that complicate it, but the air itself,
the fundament, then this, this would be it.
It coats the nose, the throat, and rings the tongue
yet leaves at its centre a void ready
to receive it as substance, as CRAB MEAT.

J

Francesco Pedraglio

And so she finally got it all off her chest and admitted she hated having to wait for J to turn up for dinner, having to put up AGAIN with his treacherous delays, his uncaring attitude, especially on weekends when it was their turn to cook, I mean, how rude of him! Not even a phone call, not even a message... and anyway that wasn't all she couldn't stand... for one thing she definitely couldn't bear that filth piling up on the living room table, those old newspapers scattered around the toilet floor with no function whatsoever other than gathering more and more hair balls around the edges, like a nauseating organic carpet flapping at the constant draft sneaking beneath the old doors of the flat... no point in mentioning those candy wrappers left on the window sill to slowly discolour like shiny dead insects unwillingly reminding her of nights spent doing nothing, absolutely NOTHING AT ALL! And what about that walking stick of his, always in the corner of her eye, the same walking stick which we all know he didn't really need any longer and why on earth was he still using it, what the hell was he trying to demonstrate with that... was he really expecting to carve out some easy fuck with it? Maybe

deceiving a poor young student into taking pity on him
and dropping on their knees to crave benediction or
extreme unction... because if that was his idea, if that
was the ingenious plan behind the whole stick business,
clearly he was wasting his worthless time, obviously it
wasn't going to happen, it really wasn't, not in a million
years! And anyway it wasn't just his filthy mind that was
disconcerting, depressing her, no... it wasn't just his cut
price, peccaminous fantasies that were getting on her
nerves... it was precisely that THING you know, that
object, the walking stick itself, with its pathetic ribbing
pattern, its cheap finish and its horribly varnished wood
that stunk from miles away of second rate charity shop—
if that was even an option—and inevitably reminded her
of the person who must have died with it or next to it or
on it, how its previous owner must have croaked suddenly
or after a painfully long disease, leaving nothing behind
for posterity other than this stupid walking stick and
possibly a dog or something similar because that's what
old people do when they die don't they? They leave
behind those kinds of things... and so why not bring back
the dog as well? Why hadn't he brought home the
fucking dog together with that idiotic stick... like some
fucking shepherd... at least it would have been an
attempt at something kind, a nice gesture, saving a life or
something, but no, not in his scheme of things, oh no...
he just went for the easiest option, the lowest common
denominator, a stick and a fuck, by hook or by crook...
like a beast! He was more than satisfied with that stick
and the potential for even an imaginary increase in
libidinous activity without ever, no, not for one minute
beginning to think creatively... well, that was his problem
you know, his absolute limit! No imagination whatsoever,
not even enough to envisage how a dog might have
afforded him one or two more opportunities on the

fantasy shagging spectrum, some random animal-loving woman or boy perhaps, I don't know... not that she wanted to help, to become some weird pimp, an accomplice in his lecherous plans, not one bit! But PLEASE not THAT object, not that stupid stupid stick... and besides, she had almost tripped over it the other night, she could have broken her neck you know... and who else would have bothered to clean up that mess of male pubic hair and scum daily clogging and befouling the shower drain? Certainly she couldn't picture him or J doing it... the two princes, the aristocrats, the *gran signori*, not really... and so she continued going on and on, until it became clear she couldn't stand lots of other things but it didn't really matter because while she was shouting out all her disgust, her rage and regret for what she considered a less than pitiful existence, he was in the kitchen, down on his knees, his face pressed against the cold white Formica, aluminium handle touching lips, his arm blindly projected forward fiddling with one of the bottom drawers where they piled up pots and oven dishes – a mess really! just like their life... A MESS— unable to hear any of what she had to say and anyway even if he could have, it didn't matter because he was far too busy trying to remember all the essential ingredients for his famous Sunday stuffed chicken, his *bird a la punk* as he liked to call it and which title was attributable to a certain freedom taken regarding both the recipe's orthodoxy and the levels of basic hygiene absent throughout the entire venture, yet nevertheless J's favourite and their sister's favourite too, even if she would never have admitted it openly, not in a million years and not in front of him... in fact, just to piss him off, she would not even have sat down to eat without first looming up there at the end of the table like some fucking Medea, a ghost at the feast, horrified, with that

inquisitive gaze of hers, contemplating the egg stains encrusting the prongs of a fork, the one between the second and the third place from the left, standing there, Eurydice turned to salt, when instead she longed to be tucking in to that succulent dish, the dish HE KNEW she loved so much, that punked-up bird he could sense she adored at least as much as he or J did and CHRIST if that annoyed him, better not to think about it, better to concentrate on preparing it all to perfection with the chopping, the cleaning, the stuffing, and anyway J would be back home soon and wasn't it a great idea to welcome him with some food ready on the table, well served and all that... I mean, for once! Even if he had skipped his turn to cook, simply not bothering to show up again and he really didn't deserve it, let's face it... I mean, not-even-a-phone-call-not-even-a-message, he could hear her screaming from the other room, but that's just J you know, that's how he is take him or leave him... and after all it's just a dinner for God's sake, just a dinner, no reason to get so irredeemably sour about it! Let's just ask him to wash up afterwards and that's will be enough... instead how nice to go on preparing it all regardless, so that their brother would get home to find a steaming chicken *a la punk*, imagine! Surely it would plant the idea in J's head that he should come back earlier next week and cook something special himself... surprise them for once... A SURPRISE for Christ sake! Just once! Enough of a reason for all of them to sit down, relax and forget about the buzzer not working, the front door needing repair, the carpet generally spotted with equivocal stains and cigarettes burns appearing more and more like a bizarre representation of the solar system and its adjacent galaxies drawn by a four year old child and less and less like the respectable floor of a good, honest, Christian home... and so while finally getting hold of what he

recognised by touch as the rectangular serving dish and while his sister was still screaming her head off about the walking stick affair, he fixed his gaze on a feeble yet steady line of grease marking the entire inner margin of that pot, a line of fat that appeared to resist consecutive attacks of both a metal sponge and the large flat head of a butter knife, so that he had nothing else to do other than engage all his powers of positive thinking to envisage in that scummy residue of one-week-old lasagna a mighty boost to today's meal, a sacred sign, an alchemic token spurring him to consequently move towards the fridge, pick up onions, garlic, rosemary and the bird itself and start the whole messy business, not before having turned the radio's volume right up to be completely sure he would not to have to listen to any more of that annoying litany about his brother's sexual habits delivered at the top of his sister's voice from next door and probably to the great enjoyment of the neighbours... and while adjusting the radio's antenna, which by the way was made up from some sort of metal wire they had torn off the trellis in Mrs Jameson's rose garden, he thought to himself how absolutely necessary it was to concentrate on his cooking right now, still keeping some mental space free for that metallic voice coming right through the crackling speaker directly into his brain, a certain Eastern European accent, Latvian maybe, most probably Lithuanian, a voice trying not without difficulties to explain the differences between time in writing and cinema making, the way it elapses differently in each medium, with cinema having the advantage of representing the concurrency of actions, as if it was ALL HAPPENING AT THE SAME TIME, almost as if we were all breathing at the same time... actually doing it now... so BREATHE NOW for Christ sake! The only exception being if we were actually dead, which doesn't

seem to be the case anyway... and everything would be perfect, just perfect, only cooking and listening and thinking, fantastic even! That was if Mrs Jameson herself, that old witch, if she hadn't decided to start banging that fucking stick of hers—another stick? what's happening here? Or was it a broom or something—on the thin partition wall dividing their kitchen and her bedroom, so that he had to point out to his sister I told you not to scream, you freak! And that old crazy lady now calling them both by their names, and how the fuck did she know their names anyway? And his sister apparently undismayed, continued her shouting while the radio voice was finally drawing some really interesting conclusion and he, knife in his hand, distracted for an instant that felt like a lifetime by a sudden dull thud coming right up from the window in front of the sink, the one facing the busy road on the north side of the building, a noise like that of heavy boxes being unloaded onto pavements, a noise distracting him just long enough to miss the explanation of the REAL difference between filmic and literary timing, his sister suddenly coming in to enquire about the noise coming from the road and did he hear that too? Or the old lady threatening to call the council... and when everything settled back to normal—shit... just a split second!—there he was once again chopping onions and crying, while she was moving the mahogany cupboard to get at a troublesome umbrella wedged in between that catafalque and the magnolia wall and Mrs Jameson doing God-knows-what in that sad little apartment of hers and the street outside now echoing with the equally confused screams of passer-by gathering beneath their window and both of them, sister and brother, both of them and possibly also Mrs Jameson and Mr Marker and the weird Polish guy living beneath them, all wondering at the same time how could people

scream that much on a Sunday morning, don't they have some respect for their neighbours? And all of them forgetting about that whole business pretty soon just to go back to their separate activities while the screams were anyway muffled by sirens and car's tires screeching on the dry asphalt and you would have thought they would have noticed it by now, would have detected that something was happening out there, but they were all too busy with their own futilities, Mr Shultz putting a folded wedge under his wobbly dinner-table with some old cardboard obtained from a birthday card sent by an aunt from Warsaw, Mrs Jameson adjusting the reclining back of a chair she bought a few weeks before, following the pressing recommendation of her osteopath, and the brother and sister lost respectively in the sound of frying aubergines and in a frantic adjusting of the sofa's cushions that were simply too soft and would always get stuck under that rim covered in crumples and lost pennies, and finally they all managed to somehow miss the ambulance, the sirens, the traffic jam producing a line of cars and angry drivers causing chaos around the entire block and still J was nowhere to be seen, how rude of him! Maybe they shouldn't have cooked for him after all, they shouldn't have thought about it in the first place... you know what, SCREW HIM, no stuffed chicken for J, chicken *a la punk* my ass, SCREW HIM! And when he finally shut up and she finally shut up too and it felt like the entire building had shut up at the very same time and the air was filled with yells and howling sirens and what the fuck is happening out there? And J was really late, absolutely, inexcusably late, and something must have happened in the street, all that traffic and all those police cars, it's not normal, and turn the oven off will you? and why has every bloody kid in the entire neighbourhood gathered opposite our front

door? And it looks like an accident... an accident happened out there... some idiot got run over! And precisely at that point... precisely at that point... precisely then, that's when the phone rang.
Well... finally a little silence!

Guess What?

Heather Phillipson

From the get-go, we went along with the whopping scam. The whole planet looked like food and all its muddy creatures our handy/cosmic pizza. We ate hungrily, because eating resembles hunting and hunting resembles love, and we just loved the heat-up-wipe-clean induction hob. We were hell-bent on love. Or lurve. Or our shoddy but realistic guesstimate of it.

Sex sex sex was reliable. Walking along corridors, filling holes with plaster, Bankers Automated Clearance Services, this was sex. Restocking our mouths was sex. Stapling documents was sex. Automated weaponry was sex. Locking and unlocking doors was sex. A particularly satisfying variant involved long-distance chat with no physical contact.

Who am I trying to kid? Excuse me while I peel my banana.

But we did have a trick up our sleeves. Putting it all down to remote control, piloted from thousands of miles away,

we could shrug off common feelings like the common cold. We could pump iron.

I'll simply die if I don't.

Duct tape, crude oils, minerals+multi-vits! Anxiety came as standard, or was it anticipation or a frisson of isolation? Quite apart from being indoors, mainly, quite apart from checking the forecast, quite apart from managing the mailbox, the wave of the future rushed our weakening thighs. We spent years pressed to the chest of boredom/waiting, then...   kerpoW!   Crematorium.

Motion is exhausting. It's a gutsy thing to keep feeling the world's movements.

And that's not really the problem anyway. There was something in the brushwork of FuckYeahNails! that reminded us of the brutal interfaces. Leopard-print lacquer was revised repeatedly. Women in face-masks attended to our chipped outer-layers. O THANX! we verbalized, because prevention of flaking was tantamount to love-making.

Do you l.o.v.e the sound of trembling in late September?

And then the handle came off my bicycle, right there in my hand, all slithery! Down I went, nosing tarmac, about-to-snuff-it, alone with a road-sign. !But what'll happen to the wet kiss never slapped on his hot lips? !I hadn't been meaning to go on about the sliminess of our situation! !How many handbags I loved and lost! !Don't dead bodies belong to others? Slouched like a bleeding ulcer on a thirsty highway, I saw larvae collecting around the pre-rotten innards. I saw my physical make-up,

proportions balanced like an aerated choc-bar with mint polyps. It wasn't easy to breathe, as usual.

Then I survived. But I hate all that bullshit. Language is like teeth which, before we let language appear, were for murdering or caressing. They too have celebrations and die.

A dentist weeps for the rubble scratching in our molars.

That's how we get so behind, the daily mega clean-up. Water, thank God, screams like brainwaves and, when it can manage it, floods a person's surfaces.

Then there's the other side of the argument. Our underpants are shrinking, partly because we're in them too deep, like the contracting continents. After the saturation and the clingy fabrics, wow the circulation bubbles like butter! And melts away.

The Death Of The Corporal, A Journey Without Luggage.

Kit Poulson

As a last resort, if Glavnauka will find it impossible to issue funds for the organisation of the exhibition or the trips of the individual heads of departments. I, as Head of the Department of Painterly Culture (Formal-Theoretical), would like to petition Glavnauka to aid me in receiving visas and credentials to facilitate my journey to France through Warsaw and Germany on foot, which I propose to begin on May 15, and reach Paris on November 1, planning to return by train on December 1.
Director of the Institute
(K. Malevich).
December 9th 1925

Have you ever walked through the farmlands between us and the border region? I doubt it, I don't think anyone has. From here you only travel one way, the shortest way to the edge. The quickest way out, then find a different route. The first settlers probably just got bogged down in the mud and had no energy to go any further. I imagine them watching the brightly caparisoned horde trundle onwards, not realising they will never rejoin it and their

descendents of a thousand years will still wonder why.

The world's spin pulls me along, rolls me into collision, as careless of my comfort as a child is of the toy tugged on the end of a string.

My boots are encased by two perfect spheres of mud. The strong thin wind keeps catching the canvas which is slung across my back and lifting me into the air. I am flying! The wind is occasionally strong enough to lift me above the level of the corn. I pop up into the sky, for a moment above the great green lake of the field. I see the truck, harnessed to a pair of carthorses. The driver, sitting on the roof of the cab, holding the reins, leaps up and points with a theatrical startlement worthy of an Eisenstein film. His companion hefts a rifle to his shoulder and puff, BANG. The bullet whistles hopelessly wide, and the man, thrown off balance by the recoil, totters for a second before falling backwards into the field. A distant shout, and a flock of wheeling birds rises up, disturbed by the event.

I drop back to the ground, my feet cycling wildly and then finding a grip. I walk onwards. They will soon catch up and resume their shadowing position. At night they overtake me.

I construct my shelter from the canvases leant together. I crawl in and feel the earth soft warm hard cradle and crave and long for flight. I dream of my escape, a passage of layers, static and consanguineous, they allow me a comet trajectory. Moving through the pages, remembered, held, my ideas stain the present, not changing the ink shapes of the words, but the paper of the actual book.

Morning, face wet from dew and body aching. Imagine a watcher surprised as my eyes suddenly flick open, my gaze spearing. But there is no one there, just the blue bowl of sky. Turning onto my side I see that they have set up their table a few feet down the road. An exhausted young soldier leans on a rifle, standing next to a striped wooden barrier. He has been up all night. He notices the movement, and shouts to someone in the truck's cab.

Where to walk but along the road, towards the barricade? A second soldier has joined the first. He is older and has obviously just awoken.

"HALT! State your name and business...

Let me see your papers... Sit in that chair and wait to be called, my superiors will need to examine these.

Keep him under surveillance."

I sit on the uncomfortable wooden chair by the roadside. The young soldier stands to one side with his gun levelled at my head, his eyelids and rifle drooping. The corporal stamps away holding the ragged stuffed envelope of documents I had handed him. Three other figures now emerge stretching from the back of the truck. They sit around a camping table and begin to consume breakfast. The corporal has placed my papers on the truck's bonnet, perhaps hoping some will be blown away, and now acts as their servant. He tends the field samovar, like some demented engine driver swathed in clouds of steam. The three do not acknowledge him, but talk loudly grasping whatever food or drink comes near to hand. My stomach moans. My body feels light, only

The Death Of The Corporal, A Journey Without Luggage.

the weight of my heavy wool coat and trousers hold me together. Air and bones, ache and dirt. I can die but I can't leave.

Finally they have finished their meal and amble towards another table that the corporal has put up in the shade of the van. One of them disappears into a small tent set a discreet distance from the camp. My bundle of papers is opened and examined. The old soldier clears away the breakfast table. A flock of small brown birds moves through the crops in front of me, hopping from stem to stem, up, down, sideways.

How many times has this happened before? Thirty, maybe forty. An impromptu rolling blockage, a sudden demand for permissions, identities, plans, assurances.

"You, here now. What is this?" A finger points at a grubby tiny reproduction of a painting of a fruit bowl.

"Is this what you are preaching?"

"Bourgeois formalist!"

"Wanker." This last muttered by the corporal.

I know these three at the table, I remember them from when they were journalists and advisors in the old days. For a while, I think even my supporters.

"You tried to shoot me again."

"An accident, comrade…"

"The corporal was alarmed by the sudden appearance of

what he took to be a counter revolutionary flying device."
"Wanker... next time we won't miss." The words spat, emphatic and quiet, from just behind my ears. The corporal's breath has a strange sweet sourness. It reminds me of sandalwood.

"Leaving without luggage." He examines my face looking for signs of fear or hopelessness that he can exploit, cracks he can prise open.

BANG. The young soldier had finally succumbed to exhaustion and let the barrel of his rifle drop down onto the ground.

"You there! To attention! You are on a charge." The young man snaps woozily back into his toy soldier stance. As the rifle comes level with my head he gives me a goofy grin. The corporal pulls a small tatty notebook from his tunic pocket and makes a mark with a pencil stub on a page already covered with similar scrawls. He finishes with a stabbed full stop, then fixes the soldier and me with a bored sneer, as if trying to commit the scene to some special part of his memory.

"Wankers." the corporal spits again then strides behind the truck towards the field toilet.

The horses which have been tethered to graze nearby, stir and paw. Moments later we hear the sound that has spooked them. A popping motorbike engine, a spot appears on the horizon, resolving itself into a cloud of dust, and then clearly a man, his machine roaring and bumping along the dirt track.

The rider is all but invisible inside a leather coat and

helmet, his eyes covered with goggles, and a scarf wrapped around mouth and nose. He seems of a piece with the heavy leather saddle bags slung on his bike, and over his shoulder.

Telegram, urgent.

The soldier does not lower his rifle, so he pushes the slip of paper into the soldier's hand, then spins back up the road, covering us with another small dust cloud. The three at the table wait for it to settle, then one of them strolls to collect the message. I know this insouciance is affected. These telegrams bring orders from Command. They are important enough to warrant the petrol denied to their truck.

As the message is read, all pretence of casualness is dropped. The face of the reader turns pale, and the message is passed to another of the three.

"For you, comrade"

I call out.

"What is it comrade? Invitation to a show trial? Demotion to the ranks? Home without luggage? Immediate accidental death?"

The three are no longer seamless, but look at each other with a horror of contamination.

"You be quiet," one squeaks at me, and then louder, "Where is the corporal?"

All eyes turn towards the small canvas construction that

is the field toilet. We realise something is wrong. The canvas bulges violently and the guy ropes strain.

"The corporal is being attacked!"

They rush toward the tent, fumbling to pull their well-polished revolvers from holsters.

"Mind you don't hurt someone with those toys."

"Private, keep that man quiet." The soldier prods me with his gun barrel.

Before they reach the tent, the whole structure topples sideways and the corporal staggers out. His trousers are round his ankles. His cap has fallen forward over his eyes. He clasps his chest and falls to the ground, taking great shuddering breaths. I wonder how many he has got left, and begin to count them. Fifteen as it happens, and then he slumps inert. His face falls into a look of bored disappointment. His penis swells into a rictus erection. None of the three has done anything but stand and watch, but now they approach.

"He is dead."

"Heart seizure or something... he never ate anything but pig fat. No man's bowels can take that."

"He drank a whole bottle of rum last night."

A pause.

"An unfortunate but natural occurrence."
This seems to satisfy their desire for a post mortem.

They confer, shooting anxious glances first at me, then at the body.

"We need to go to the next town and telegram a report. This is urgent. We must do it by the book…"
"Maybe they will give us some petrol."
"What about the telegram?"
"You'll soon find out about that…"
"To town, get the private to harness the horses… and this…"
"Get the private to bury him?"
"There are tests, papers…"
"I suppose you had better wrap him up soldier, use the canvas from the tent."

"And him?"
"Let him go. I don't want to be out in the sun with this… with him, if you see what I mean.
We will catch up with him later."

The young soldier still has his gun levelled at me and gives me another conspiratorial smirk. I turn away and begin to walk along the road.

The Angels in this Place are Unrecognizable

Chris Sharp

Chapter 2

"I saw the Google Car," James said, sitting across from Rach' on his first morning back. He was wearing a white v-neck t-shirt, boxers. It was a bright and warm spring morning in New York. Their small, well-ordered, but expensive West Village flat was filled with sunlight from a wall of windows that looked out onto terraces and rooftops. Beyond that, the Hudson. Jersey. She was wearing her long white skirt, a pale blue tank top. Nappy, red bed-head hair. Her entire being redolent with sleep. With woman waking from sleep. She looked at him with her green eyes and her slightly bird-like nose, which gave her soft features an avian character. Far from being a defect, this slight imperfection only enhanced her beauty in his mind.

"The Google Car," he insisted. "I saw the Google Car three days ago in Paris."

"What's the Google Car?" she sipped her coffee.

"You don't know what the Google Car is?"

She gave him a blank look.

"The Google Car." He said, surprised by her ignorance. Rach' was generally more informed than he was. Usually it was the other way around; her explaining things, recent innovations, politics, etc., to him. He continued: "Nine eyes. They circulate all over the world. Mapping it. Taking photos. Google street view is generated by the Google Car. The ubiquitous, all seeing and unseen Google Car."

This seemed to pique her interest.

"I think," He said, realizing it as he said it. "I'm the only person I know who has ever seen it." As if it were the last unicorn. The Loch Ness monster. Some mythical beast. Or as if it were one car. A single, mutant automobile, which managed to multiply itself without ever forfeiting its singularity. And not hundreds. Or maybe thousands that restlessly roam the earth. Imaging it. And continually uploading it onto servers. Replicating it with inhuman accuracy. Instantly and miraculously generating a microcosmic cartography of the world of which cartographers of yore would have never even dreamed. That would have blown their cartographic minds. Into tiny bits. Archipelagos of incomprehension.

"Really?"

He thought about it for a moment. Trying to remember if he'd known anyone who'd ever seen it. "Yes, I don't know anyone. Which is funny, if you think about it. It's like being blessed. Seeing something special. Like seeing behind the curtain." He paused. "Like seeing god, the eye of god, or something."

"What did it look like?" She asked avidly.

"A small, white car. Rather nondescript. But a kind of hexagon or something sticking out of its roof on

a pole. A hexagon full of cameras. Like a big knob, hock, or fist covered with cameras. 'Google Car' painted on the side. I don't know. It was going really fast actually."

She was already opening her lap top, presumably googling it. He moved around the table to join her on the side. They studied the Google Car in a rapt silence. Skipping around pages. Wikipedia. Articles. Images. They learned about the various versions. Depending on where in the world you were it varied. He must have seen the Subaru Impreza. Or something like it (had he actually ever seen a Subaru in France? He wondered. No idea, this was not necessarily the kind of information that he registered on a daily basis, car makes, etc). With a blown up detail of a Google map superimposed on its white exterior, the green doors with "Google Maps Street View" in white on the side. It seemed oddly cheerful, friendly, harmless. They learned of the existence of the Google snowmobile. The Google trike. Developed and deployed for those hard to reach spots. Such as alleyways, mountain tops. There was an image of the trike, which looked like a kind of ice cream tricycle such as you used to see in Central Park, riderless and parked in front of la Fontana di Trevi in Rome. Not a soul in sight. Odd. And highly improbable.

"So this is Street View?" It clicked for her.

"Exactly," he affirmed. "This is how it's done. Cars. Snowmobiles and trikes."

"Amazing that I have never seen one."

"No one I know has ever seen one."

"Have you looked for yourself yet?"

He paused a moment before responding, "No."

She was already typing in Paris, France, when she asked, "Where were you?"

"Oberkampf. La rue Oberkampf."

"What were you doing up there?"

"Here zoom in, because I can't remember the exact name of the street."

They skipped the cursor around the grid. Dragging it. Shifting Paris around. He recognized the cross section, which was actually a park. A nameless park. The street itself was La rue Jean Aicard. Who was Jean Aicard? No idea.

"Here, La rue Jean Aicard," He pronounced it with difficulty. It wasn't a name that rolled off the tongue. It didn't like being there. "I was at an opening," he explained. "Bad. Bad show, but nice night."

It was a nice night. One of those nights. But maybe it was not quite night yet, but rather twilight. The gloaming. Which is the best night. The best of night. The promise of night. Evening rather. A splendid evening. A bit balmy. It was one of those indeterminate evenings when it could have been spring or fall. Transitional. In-between somehow. One or the other. Or both. Soft. And patinated. The dwindling light mediated by so many textured surfaces. Hues. The trees. The pavement. The striations and scuffs on walls. People standing on corners. Like so many colors. You gaze around at the vivid world—because it is vivid, everything so vivid, as if just after a fresh rain—and you feel lucky to be alive. Grateful. To be taking in so much. Of the vivid, beautiful world. Even if, little do you know, an event, i.e., an "event," of which you are not even remotely cognizant, of which you will only become retrospectively cognizant because some obscure, unfathomable order has deemed it so, is about to occur, and radically alters the course of your life. But nevertheless, you walk home thinking that it is a beautiful night. Such a beautiful night. But this, you will soon learn, he was to soon learn, was only a version of that night, or evening, or twilight, or what have you. Which would be replaced by another version.

Or maybe a couple of different versions.

"Oh my god," Rach's voice seemed to go up an octave. "There you are!"

And it was true. He had been uploaded. There he was. Standing on the sidewalk. Alone. Apparently looking directly at it. It? One of the cameras. One of the nine. His quizzical looking figure. Standing there not so much as a question mark, but an exclamation mark. Emphatically puzzled in his dark green pants. White button-up shirt. You could even make out his mustache and goatee, despite his blurred out face (all the faces were blurred out, that's Google, that's the so-called respect for privacy, the right thereto, there was an algorithm built especially for this, to blur out faces). He was watching. Watched. Witnessing the passage. Presumably stunned by just such a passage. Shocked. The Google Car. You could almost see it, read it on his blurred out face: "That's the fucking Google Car."

Rach' shifted the view, wanting, he suspected, to see him from another angle. She moved the arrow out into the street so that the point of view would be out on the street looking in at the sidewalk (which is where he must have first spotted it). Everything momentarily went out of focus. Blurring by. Like an unsuccessful tracking shot. Or as if all the molecules (his included) suddenly went slack, lifting up and pulling apart, and then suddenly dropped back into place, cohering into clarity. And there he was. From a different angle. Watching as he was watched. Behind him the nameless park. A telephone stand. A garbage can. Green, leafy trees.

"What is that?" Rach' asked.

"What is what?" he asked, looking at the image.

"That," she pointed with her finger. A few meters behind the fence there was a man in a suit. He seemed to be bending over to pick something up.

Kneeling to pray. But one arm raised. Or maybe he was falling. Waving at someone? Hello or goodbye? Hello and goodbye?

"I don't know, I didn't remember seeing him. In fact, I didn't see him. I saw the Google Car. Was too preoccupied by the uniqueness of such a sighting to pay attention to my surroundings."

"Look at his head."

He looked. It seemed extraordinarily blurry. Much more blurry than, say, James' (still in the foreground). As if a certain number of molecules had actually detached themselves from his skull. Definitively pulling it apart.

"Oh my god J," Rach' gasped. "I think that's blood. Or brain?"

He looked closer. "Can you zoom in?"

They did, or tried, but in the next image, they were presumably standing on top of the fallen man, and he was gone. No where to be seen. They zoomed back out, returning to the same bewildering and relatively interpretable image. Absorbing it for a few moments in silence.

"What do you think?" She asked him. Her breathing was growing short. A tension had filled the room, the morning. A sudden musk.

"If this were a movie," James reasonably reasoned, despite his perplexity at the turn the morning was taking. "We would pan around the surrounding buildings. Looking for something. Some sign. A clue. The barrel of a gun."

"Totally," Rach' seemed to squirm. He knew that squirm. That unease. The way she moved. He heard something in her body crack. Like her ankle. As if she wearing stretching it.

"Zoom around to the left," he ordered. She

did. Shifting in her seat next to him. The buildings, the
street blurred by. In a state of subdued, but mounting
panic, he became distracted, suddenly imagined himself
unceremoniously bending her over the counter, pulling
her skirt up above her hips and sliding himself directly
into her. Which is basically what he did a few minutes
later. But with a little more ceremony. I.e., short of
breath, she lifted her leg up and propped her foot on the
seat of her chair, spreading her alabaster, white legs, like
a casual, but deliberate invitation. Although calculated,
her desire felt no less animal and sharp than his, he could
all but smell it, radiating outward from her womanhood.
She looked at his body, taking it in. His solid, cut figure
clad in a white t-shirt and red boxers, which did nothing
to conceal his growing erection. They didn't even look
at each other, as if it out of shame. Continuing to stare
at the image in front of them, apparently mesmerized
by it, as if this wasn't actually happening, none of this
was happening (he actually thought that, thought: "This
isn't happening.") He placed his hand on the inside of
her ankle and ran it up along the inside of her creamy,
slightly chubby thigh, stopping just before the end,
gazing down at her legs as her long skirt slowly rose up.
He leaned forward and briefly placed his mouth on her
collarbone, sucking on the base of her neck. He then
directed her off the chair, around the table to the kitchen
counter, and gently but firmly bent her over. She, all the
while, submitting, without even looking at him, gazing
impassively (culpably?) at the floor. The sound of a body
being driven into a counter top. Dishes moving. Rippling
out of the way. His hand cupped around her. Her wetness
lathering into her pubic hair. His fingers briefly inside
of her, they groaned together as he slide himself into
her and almost exploded. But something wasn't quite
right, was slightly off. Generally, when they made love,

the depth and seeming vastness of their physical and emotional connection invariably took on a miraculous quality, felt, in fact, like a miracle. Making love with her was miracle. But not now, not this time. There seemed to be some kind of edge, some unwanted veneer of privacy, as if each were immured in his and her self. But so novel was this experience, so strange was it that he didn't panic. He felt more fascinated by it, more like a spectator at his own disjuncture, while nevertheless pumping into her, trying to find his way fully and completely into her. And failing. Fascinated by this failure.

Afterwards, they lay there, hunched over the counter, he on top of her, at once shocked and thrilled by the brutality of their symmetrically shared desire- a desire saturated with an illicitness, due to its potentially homicidal origins (potentially?). Or maybe they were cinematic. The origins.

"Or maybe something even stranger than that," he later wondered, half out loud to himself, also wondering if they should talk about it, or let it remain, strange, alien, raw and unassimilated, in the receding foreground of their shared psyche. The shared psyche of their relationship. Perhaps it is better to leave certain mysteries intact. Maybe that's what keeps a given relationship green, fresh. The irruption and relative preservation of such events. But it was hard to ignore that there was something dark and unwieldy about it, something portentous and unsettling.

Later that afternoon, after they recovered from that demonic erotic episode, and had taken a nap (one of the naps that had become indispensable and ritual to their reunions), they returned to the images. Almost casually, as if they were of little or no importance. A curiosity. To see if they could put the pieces together. Or properly take them apart. Or make them add up. He was

making coffee when he heard Rach' behind him, "Oh my god babe; he's gone."

Is it too fatalistic for James to expect that? Is this a betrayal of his fundamentally sanguine character? Or can such optimism and seemingly fatalistic irony co-exist? In certain persons, in the 21st century, yes. Of course he's gone, thought James. He knew he would be gone. Entire swathes of history, some of the most significant novels and films of the twentieth century had trained him to expect this. He had to be gone. His erasure was inevitable. It could be no other way. As if even he, the man in the suit himself knew it. Knew that even this incidental registration of his death (or what they presumed to be his death) would be smudged out, withdrawn from perceivable and verifiable circulation and summarily chucked into the virtual ether. Maybe that was why he was waving goodbye. The double goodbye. Goodbye and goodbye.

"What do you mean? You're fuckin' with me."

"I mean," she sounded seriously appalled, terrified. Rach' couldn't invent this. The note of despair in her voice was real. Genuine. Bona fide. "He's gone."

He turned around. "Am I still there?"

"Yes babe, but he's gone."

Letter #2 (Gratitude)

David Steans

My name is David Steans and this statement - no, this request - is addressed towards my fellow artists. You have all given me so much—and so freely!—that it pains me to ask of you again. Innumerable gifts and offerings. But ask of you again I must. I can't repay you in kind—it would take a hundred lifetimes to reciprocate—but perhaps a few well-chosen words can express my grateful sentiments. So, please, indulge me in a capricious daydream and remember that my heart, full of love, feels like it's in the right place.

I wish that we could all live together, permanent residents of a spacious art gallery-cum-project space-cum-studio complex.

I wish my legs were the length of ladders, and could stretch and bend like rubber snakes; arms just as long, like endless coils of rope. I would hang myself across the gallery like a giant hammock, calmly and contentedly awaiting the close, thick night. At day's end everybody would pack away their